THE HOLLOWAY HOAX

THE BLAIR GRAVES FILES
BOOK 2

MARNIE VINGE

For all of you that have experienced something you can't quite explain.
Keep searching.

CHAPTER ONE

I STAND at the picture window in the upstairs bedroom I designated as a holding space for my father's things. Surrounded by dusty filing cabinets and strange artifacts, I hold one such relic in my hands. A photo album. I went to look for my camera, but didn't find it. I'm not sure why I thought it was in here to begin with. It didn't take long before I dipped my hand into one box I'd sworn I would go through as part of my New Year's resolutions.

I drew out a photo album, and now I'm staring at my mother's face. I trace the line of her jaw through the cellophane that covers the late nineties album. There are pictures of me and Blake at birthday parties. Both our own and at other's. Most of them little friends that have been long forgotten in the weathering of time.

Some of them, though, are of Noelle and me. The

one friend that I've been able to hold on to all these years.

The photo of my mother is a close-up, taken by my father, likely a year or two before she died. A year or two before Blake and I were born. She died unexpectedly during childbirth. It was fast and my dad was ill-prepared for such a premature loss. He never elaborated on it any more than that. I suppose as a kid—and as an adult—I saw little purpose in figuring out more about it.

Now, with him legally dead, his house off the market, and me living it what was once one of the most famous homes in Oklahoma, it's the first time I've slowed down enough to give it some thought. It's been on my mind lately. Today, going up here to get the camera, and not finding it, I guess my subconscious got me to stay in here, surrounded by my father's things.

Surrounded by the past.

My dad never put out photos of my mom when Blake and I were younger. It was like he thought he could protect us from the loss of her if he kept it to himself. As if it wasn't a blow suffered by all of us.

He kept everything to himself, allowing no one else to shoulder the weight, even for a moment.

The thought saddens me.

I should be perky, peppy, and excited for the road trip that awaits. And just as that thought is occurring to me, I hear tires on gravel and the rumble of a V8 engine in my drive.

I snap the album shut and look up. I see Cash's pickup truck coming up to the house.

He pulls into the circle drive and gets out then heads for the front door. I shove the album back into the cardboard moving box it came out of. I'll go back for it when we get home.

Cash Kelly, the supernaturally interested YouTube sensation, has offered to take me for a four-day getaway.

Okay, maybe that's a little romanticized. He's letting me tag along on a trip to a Bigfoot festival that promises a good deal of paranormal hijinks.

Or at least some presentations by the most prominent researchers in the field today.

I give up my search for my camera. The one on my phone will have to do. I jog down the stairs, going as quickly as my short legs allow, and then I hear his knock at the door.

"Coming!" I shout. I grab the handle and swing the door wide.

Cash stands there, shades on, a black leather jacket and a heather gray t-shirt on over faded blue jeans and boots that look like they've spent a fair amount of time searching the woods for Bigfoot and his cronies. He looks the part for the weekend. I hope I do, too. I'm wearing a sweater, jeans, and boots, as instructed by my host.

"You ready to go?" Cash asks, tilting down his sunglasses, revealing his icy blue eyes.

I imagine he could have used those in another life as a detective. They have a soul-piercing quality to them, even I have to admit.

"Ready as I'll ever be," I tell him.

He steps inside and grabs my bags.

"Hey!" I say. "I can get those."

"My Daddy taught me never to let a woman carry her own luggage," he says as he heads back across the lawn to the circle drive where he loads it all into the back of the truck.

"Thanks," I mutter under my breath as I close the door and lock it behind me after grabbing my purse from the coatrack.

I hot foot it out to the truck. Cash is already inside by the time I climb up and close my door. He's got the heat cranked up, something I'm grateful for. It's an overcast day with a high of thirty-six degrees Fahrenheit.

The walk from the house to the car was enough to put a chill on my bones. It occurs to me we haven't really established how much time we might spend in the great outdoors over the next four days.

"What's the plan?" I ask as Cash heads for the main road. I glance back at the house once, like I always do when I'm leaving, wondering if I turned everything off even though I know I did.

The house has seemed more empty lately. Which makes sense, seeing as how Cash helped me rid it of a rather sad ghost over the holidays. Her unfinished business is now finished and I miss her.

Somehow the house felt more full with her in it. Or maybe it was because Cash was coming over every night to help me resolve things. Maybe that was what made the house feel full.

I know one thing, though. I want that feeling back.

I want a crowded table and a house full of people. I want laughter and love in that house. My current status as a single woman with no prospects makes it hard to imagine a future where my table is full.

Cash heads for the highway as he answers me.

"Well, we're staying with my friend Clayton and his wife, Lisa," He pauses, concentrating on merging, then continues. "He's an old buddy of mine. A huge Bigfoot guy, too. Really into the stuff. He'll definitely go with us to all the festival events. I'm not sure if Lisa will. She's about eight months pregnant."

"Eight months pregnant?" I ask. "Are you sure they're up to hosting us?"

"She swore they were. She was the one that suggested it. And Lisa is in her element when she's the hostess. She probably hasn't gotten to do a lot of that since they moved down southeast."

I nod, silently agreeing though I know nothing about Lisa other than what Cash is telling me right now.

However, I'm sure she doesn't want to host two guests when she's nine months pregnant. If she does, she's a better woman than I am. I'd have told Cash to kick rocks.

I did my due diligence researching the event, but the website was pretty rudimentary. It has a few pictures and a line up from last year. It hadn't been updated for this one. When I looked on social media, I wasn't able to find too much about it either. But what I did find screamed off the grid militia people will be in attendance! So a social media footprint would be shallow for the event.

"So what's your friend like?" I probe, wondering if Clayton falls into that category. And his wife, too.

"He's alright," Cash says. "They moved down there when they bought a weed farm. So that's what he does. Lisa is planning on staying home with the baby once it comes."

"You know," I say. "When I was in high school, I wouldn't have known who to even ask about buying weed. Now there's a dispensary on every corner." Right across from the ubiquitous pharmacies and churches. Medical marijuana is booming in Oklahoma.

"I knew exactly who to ask," Cash says, looking over at me with a smile. "I never pegged you for such a straight arrow, Blair."

"Well, I sort of fell into that role. Blake knew all the places to score weed and God knows what else."

"So you're the good kid," Cash says, more conclusion than question. Like he's putting together a puzzle about me.

"You could say that," I offer.

"Well, it's been a long time since I've smoked weed," Cash says. "Somehow, weed and the paranormal just don't mix."

"What is it? Are you afraid a demon might possess you in your inebriation?" I tease.

"Something like that," Cash says with a smirk. "Really," he goes on. "it's more that you just want all your senses functioning at their best. Like this weekend. Smoke a joint and you're gonna see Sasquatch for certain."

"Good point," I tell him.

"Blake still doing drugs?" he asks, his tone ginger.

"Who knows?" I say. "Blake doesn't tell me anything. I think his major problem is gambling, though."

Cash makes a non-committal noise and we leave it at that for the time being. I rest my forehead on the glass of the passenger side window and wonder what, exactly, I'm in store for down here.

CHAPTER TWO

WE DRIVE until I feel like we've used up all the highway in Oklahoma and then we head south on the second leg of the journey. Our compass points in a southeastern direction, toward the corner of the state. We pass the time in companionable silence, something I hadn't given Cash credit for knowing how to do. After an hour, he breaks the silence.

"Would you do me a favor?" he asks.

"Sure," I say.

"Look up the lineup for the festival really quick," he says.

"I just check it yesterday," I tell him. "They still hadn't updated it from last year's lineup."

"I know. I just checked it yesterday, too. But I talked to Charlie Moore, the guy in charge of it, and he acted like it had slipped his mind and told me he'd make sure it got updated by today."

I pull my phone out of my back pocket and look it up. Just as it was yesterday, and the day before that, the lineup wasn't current.

"Any luck?" Cash asks.

"Looks the same as it has for the last few days," I tell him.

He grunts, obviously irritated by my answer.

"What's wrong?" I ask him.

"Well," he starts. "That makes me think old Harrison Holloway is going to be there. I had a conversation about it with Charlie. Told him it wasn't a good idea. But he and Harrison go way back."

"Who is Harrison Holloway, and why is it a bad idea?" I feel lost. Although niche drama, even if it's about Bigfoot—scratch that—especially if it's about Bigfoot, is my favorite kind.

"Harrison Holloway pulled off one of the biggest hoaxes in the Bigfoot world in the early 2000s. Footage that was better than the Patterson-Gimlin film."

"What's the Patterson-Gimlin film?" I ask, realizing there's a lot I don't know about the world of Bigfoot. Maybe I should have done more research going into this.

"The Patterson-Gimlin film is the most famous Bigfoot footage of all time. You've seen it even if you don't think you have. It's the footage that you think of instantly when someone says they caught Bigfoot on film. They shot it in California in the sixties. A creature walks across a creek bed in front of two guys who happened to catch it. There have been all kinds of hoax allegations about it by people that thoroughly researched it and even a guy who claims to have been the one in the Bigfoot suit. But it's still considered one of the cornerstone pieces of Bigfoot evidence in existence."

"So this guy Holloway pulled off some footage that was even more compelling than that?" I ask, putting the pieces together.

"Correct," Cash says. "And he's been trying to restore his name for the last few years. Turns out it's not much fun when everyone kicks you out of the sandbox."

"And Charlie is his friend?" I ask.

"Yes," Cash says. "And this is Charlie's first year as the director of the festival. Rumors have been going around that Holloway has been doing real research. I wouldn't be surprised if old Charlie scored him a place to share it at the festival."

"And you think because Charlie hasn't updated the website, that might be the case?" I ask.

Cash nods, his eyes on the road.

"Bingo," he says. "Seeing Holloway's name on the roster would scare some folks off immediately. And these are big tourist dollars for Hobby Hollow."

"What will happen if he lets Harrison Holloway give a presentation?" I ask.

Suddenly, my mind is full of various scenarios in which dramatic scenes play out at this festival. I adore hearing about niche drama, but I have no desire to be involved in it.

"I don't know," Cash says. "Something. Maybe nothing. But I imagine people will be upset about it. The community hasn't really accepted him back into their fold. He might have a friend in Charlie, but a lot of people are reluctant to toss their lot in with Holloway's because it might discredit their own research down the line." He's silent for a moment. "Plus, I don't put it past him to pull something similar now or even sometime soon."

"Is there a lot of money in Bigfoot hoaxing?" I ask, my mouth threatening to turn up in a smile. To an outsider, I have to admit that it seems silly. Despite what I just experienced in my home, this is another level of the paranormal and I'm not ready to give in to believing just yet. Ghosts are one thing. This gets you laughed out of the psych ward.

"You'd be surprised," Cash says, then glances over at me, apparently hearing the amusement in my voice. "Some people take this stuff deadly seriously."

I look back at my phone and go back to the search I did for the festival's schedule. The second article catches my eye. A missing person. I tap on it and read.

Hobby Hollow Man Still Missing — An Oklahoma man is still missing after a large search performed by local sheriff's deputies and volunteers. High school teacher Michael Berkley, 28, went missing six weeks ago. During a frigid search, authorities weren't able to find any evidence of the man. Many students from the Hobby Hollow High School took part and expressed concern for their teacher. "We just want him back," student Andy Bell said. Though Berkley remains missing, friends and family hope that they will find him.

"You hear about this?" I ask Cash.

He glances over at my phone, still driving and unable to take a moment to read what's on the screen.

"What?" he asks and turns his focus back to the road. "We're about an hour out now," he adds.

"Good to know," I say, then press on with the news story. "There's a guy missing down in Hobby Hollow. Isn't that where we're going?" Again, I chastize myself for not paying closer attention to the details of the long weekend.

Maybe I focused on other pertinent information about it.

"It is," Cash says. He sits up straighter in his seat. "Who went missing?"

"A high school teacher. Michael Berkley. Apparently well-loved by the community," I say.

"How did he go missing?" Cash asks.

"The article I was reading didn't say," I tell him. "I'll look."

I go back to my phone and look Michael up directly. The first article is the one I just read, but there are others below it, dating back to the beginning of December. About six weeks ago. The time that he first went missing.

I summarize what I find for Cash.

"It looks like he had a part-time job," I tell him. "It says he was last seen there and that his pickup truck was left there. He took his wallet and anything else important with him," I say. I scan the rest of the article. "That's about all I can tell."

Cash makes an affirmative sound.

"Do people go missing down there a lot?" I ask.

"It's a small town. Tiny. I wouldn't think so. And if they do, I would imagine it's at the hands of another person who calls that place home."

"Or Bigfoot," I suggest.

Cash gives me a sarcastic smile.

"She's got jokes, ladies and gentlemen."

"I'll be here all week," I say. "Literally."

With it being mid-January, night is still falling quickly. At around 5:45 pm, the sun is setting in the sky and both of us have shed our sunglasses.

"We're almost there," Cash announces when we leave the highway for some smaller roads.

The forest here is vast, seeming to swallow up the

land on either side of the road. Evergreens stretch upward and they bury the sun behind them, leaving Cash and me on the road in a blue twilight. The trees are so dense and so close to the road that if I got out of the truck and walked twenty-five yards into the woods, I'd be lost. The thought sends a chill up my spine and makes me think of Michael Berkley.

Surely someone who lived down here would know a thing or two about the woods. But people went missing in the woods all the time. Regardless of how much experience they'd had with them. No one was a match for the terrain of the Earth. Especially in densely forested areas.

Maybe he went missing in the woods. Maybe he would turn up. But then my mind goes back to what Cash said and I think about the possibility that someone wanted him to go missing. Maybe they wanted him to go missing so badly that they saw to it. And here we are, headed down into this tiny community, perhaps to be in the company of a murderer.

Cash makes several turns, leading us deeper and deeper into the mountainous country that makes up southeastern Oklahoma.

I keep my face pressed against the glass, peering out into the woods. Suddenly, in the newly fallen darkness, the idea of Bigfoot doesn't seem so far-fetched.

Finally, after what seems like an eternity, Cash makes a turn off of the paved road for a gravel one. I glance out the windshield and see their mailbox passing by.

The property is wooly, with overgrown greenery. I'm not sure that I would have seen the gate if I hadn't known where to look. Finally, we emerge and a house stands in the distance.

Cash pulls into the drive and I make out two people on the front porch.

"We're here," he says.

CHAPTER THREE

CASH PARKS the truck and we both hop out. I close my door and the sound echoes around us. We truly seem to be in the middle of nowhere, which was Noelle's assessment of where I told her I was going.

There's just enough light left in the sky to cast a pale purple across the front yard, which is hidden from the road both by distance and a small grove of trees. I see Clayton and Lisa on the front porch, a wraparound on their two-story ranch house. It looks new, and it looks nice. A luxury home just judging from the exterior and the pool I can see from my vantage point in the driveway.

Lights from inside illuminate both of their silhouettes.

Lisa is very pregnant. I can't imagine that she'd want to have guests right now, but I'm hoping she told Cash the truth.

"There you are!" she shouts from the porch and waves at Cash. He heads over and I follow slowly behind him, approaching carefully, the way you do when it's obvious a group of people know each other extremely well, making you feel like a bit of an outsider from the get-go.

"Hey there, you son of a bitch," Clayton says, wrapping Cash in a hug and slapping his back.

"We're so glad you're here," Lisa says to him.

I hang back.

"This is Blair," Cash says, turning to me. I step forward and extend a hand to my host for the next few days.

"Hi," I say.

"The famous Blair graves," Clayton says. He wears a baseball cap pulled tightly against his head. Clayton is almost as tall as Cash, which is saying something. He wears a Carhart coat and jeans with a pair of dirty brown boots that look like they probably have steel toes.

"Ignore him," Lisa says, taking my attention off of Clayton and redirecting it to her.

I smile and chuckle nervously, feeling a little out of place. Like the three of them are in their own orbit and I'm an interloper, circling around them, viewing it from the outside.

Lisa is short. Not as short as I am. She's a few inches taller. Beautiful brown hair that looks like it's directly out of a Herbal Essences commercial circa the mid-nineties. It falls in layers, thick and shiny. I'm instantly jealous of her.

"I'll try," I say, offering her a friendly smile. "I'm hardly famous," I say to Clayton, attempting to establish some rapport.

"Your Daddy was," he says. "That's close enough for this festival you're gonna be at this weekend," he adds.

It washes over me like ice water. The shock. I wasn't expecting it. And I hadn't even considered this: that people here this weekend might know who I was just because of my father, Graham Graves, the famed paranormal radio host that went missing seven years ago.

I glance at Cash, wondering if the dread shows on my face. But he only offers me a smile, so I don't think he catches it.

"You guys are probably ready to get inside and have something to drink," Lisa offers.

I nod my head, eager to shift the subject away from my father. It's a prickly topic for me and probably not the best thing to discuss in front of practical strangers if I'm trying to make a good impression.

"You don't have to ask me twice," Cash says with a grin. He claps his hands together and rubs them like an excited child. It makes me wonder, with his family situation, just how much time he gets like this with people he cares about.

"Let's go," Clayton says, then the four of us head for the front door.

"Hell of a place you've got here," Cash says, looking up for a second at the front of the house. I do the same. It really is nice.

"Weed farming will do that," Clayton says, grabbing the door handle. Lisa steps in and Clayton waves an arm, ushering me inside. Then he and Cash follow.

The interior of the house reminds me of something out of a country and western home decorating magazine. It's chic and calls to mind ideas about rugged men working out on the ranch. It's obvious that they've either put a lot of thought into their decor or a lot of money, paying someone else to do it. Either way, it's gorgeous, warm, and inviting.

"Wow," Cash says, echoing the thoughts running through my mind. I fight the urge to reach out to touch a stuffed bobcat sitting near the entryway.

"Thanks, man," Clayton says. "Lisa and the decorator are responsible."

I glance at Lisa, and she smiles, her cheeks blushing slightly.

"You did good," Cash tells her. I can tell there's awe in his voice. It's obvious that he hasn't seen them in a while. He didn't seem familiar with the house at all, and now this. It occurs to me I didn't ask Cash where he knew Clayton and Lisa from. I wonder if they used to live in the city. It makes me wonder if Cash has any aspiration to move out to the middle of nowhere. The thought makes me sad before I can guard myself against it. I shake it off, coming back to the present.

"Let me get you guys something to drink," Lisa says.

"Please, let me help you," I tell her, glancing at her stomach.

She heads for the kitchen and I follow her.

"We're so glad that you guys came down," Lisa says. "The festival just wouldn't be the same without Cash. And he's told us about you, Blair," she adds with a smirk that makes me blush.

"All good, I hope," I offer with a nervous laugh. Lisa's smirk deepens as she reaches up into the cabinet for some glasses.

"What would you like?" she asks. "We have wine, beer, tea, water. You name it."

"I'll take some water," I tell her, not wanting to chance getting tipsy with strangers. Especially not if they might bring my dad up all over again. You'd think the guy had written me out of his will or something with the way I am about him. But sometimes neglect is as powerful as abuse. In fact, I'm pretty sure it's the same thing, though I have no desire to go unpack that with a therapist.

"You got it," Lisa says.

"I can get it," I tell her and she hands me the glass with a smile, grateful for my help, I think. I wonder how much Clayton actually helps her with things around here. If he's like a lot of old-fashioned good ol' boys, the answer might be not much. I reserve my judgment, though. I just met them. They seem like nice people. And Cash vouched for them. I trust him.

I go to the fridge and get some ice from the dispenser and water following that. Sipping out of the crystal glass, and judging by the surrounding house, it really is real crystal.

"What do you guys want?" Lisa calls into the living room.

"Beer," Clayton calls back. She heads to the fridge and grabs a couple of longneck bottles. She pops the caps off with a bottle opener and I take one of them from her.

"I really can help while we're here," I tell her. "And he'll pull his weight, too," I say, gesturing into the living room to indicate Cash.

"Thank you," Lisa says. "I really am glad to have you guys here. It's not an imposition, really."

"Are you sure?" I ask. "You're eight months pregnant," I tell her. Then I realize the only way I know that is because Cash told me. I feel self-conscious. Like maybe I shouldn't have said that. Jesus. Why do I care so much about making a good impression on these people?

Before I can explore that train of thought, Lisa gestures as if to dismiss my concern.

"I'm fine," she tells me. "Honestly. If I have to sit around and not do anything, I'll go crazy."

I nod, hoping she's telling me the truth.

I follow her back into the living room where Cash and Clayton are engaged in the tale of how Clayton killed the deer mounted over the fireplace.

"He was a strong one," Clayton is saying as we approach. Lisa hands him his beer, and he takes it almost without looking, like they anticipate each other's every move. I wonder what that's like.

I tap Cash on the shoulder and he turns, almost surprised.

"Oh," he says. "Thank you."

He clears his throat and we make eye contact. I smile at him. I like it here. Maybe it's Lisa's warmth. But maybe I'm getting a brief glimpse into more of the things that matter to Cash. He takes his beer and I take a sip of my water. The four of us stand in front of the massive hearth and the even more massive buck mounted above.

The conversation dies down until we're all just standing there. The exhaustion of our journey hits me, and I yawn.

"Excuse me," I say. "Long day."

"Yeah, y'all probably want to get to bed early tonight. You want to order a pizza?" Clayton asks Lisa.

"Sounds good to me," she says.

"You call it in and we'll go pick it up," Clayton offers, including Cash in that.

CHAPTER FOUR

AFTER THE GUYS get back with pizza, we all gather around the beautiful wooden dining table that conjures to mind dinners on a Wyoming ranch. It's long. Big enough to fit twelve people. The spread is simple. Pepperoni pizza and ranch dressing, some cheesy bread and a couple of two liter bottles of soda that Clayton and Cash grabbed at the last minute at the pizza joint.

"I'm surprised Hobby Hollow has a pizza place," Cash says after swallowing a large bite of pepperoni pizza. I take a bite of my own, a little surprised at that, too. I haven't seen the town yet, but just from everything Cash has told me, it has to be tiny.

"Coming up in the world," Clayton says with a laugh. "It got put in around the time that the weed farm got some traction."

"What's that been like?" Cash asks, again voicing a question that I want to ask myself.

"Good," Clayton says. Then after a bite, he goes on. "Strange. What with Michael going missing. Did you hear about that up there in the city.?"

I recognize the name instantly. The guy from the article. The high school teacher.

"I did," I speak up. "Or at least I read about it on the way down here." Cash says nothing before the words are out of my mouth. The three of them look at me. "All I know is that there's a high school teacher missing," I say.

"Well, he was an employee of mine on the farm. Part-time," Clayton says. "Did the article you read tell you where his truck was found?"

I shake my head and glance over at Cash. There's an intensity to what Clayton is saying that I don't like.

"They found it at the farm," he says. "So the place was crawling with sheriff's deputies for a week of tow."

"Jesus," Cash says. "You didn't mention that when I called asking to come down. If it's a bad time-"

"Hell, the search is over. His family needs to accept that he's gone," Clayton says.

"You don't know that, honey," Lisa interjects. "If it was you missing, I'd keep searching until I found a body." She looks over at me and offers a smile. Trying to make a dark topic more palatable, I assume.

"Why do you think he went missing?" I ask. It might be rude but I want to know.

"Hell if I know," Clayton says, leaning back in his chair, done with dinner. "Some of these people that come and work on the farm get mixed up in stuff other than weed."

"I take it since the police are done with their search, your operation is legitimate," Cash says. There's a playfulness in his voice. For a moment, it makes me wonder what all I don't know about Cash and his past. Or Clayton, who I know even less about to begin with.

"Of course," Clayton says, almost defensively. Almost too quickly. "But there's no telling what some of those guys get up to on the side. There's a lot of money in weed grows, and we have one of the best operations in the state. Who knows what they spend their money on when they get off work."

"So you think it might be drug-related?" I ask.

"It's the only thing we can think of," Lisa interjects. "Drugs make people do stupid things and associate with shady characters."

I fight the urge to ask who the shady characters are in town. Immediately Harrison Holloway comes to mind. But I don't think he's a local, or the sort of shady that's out there making folks disappear. Then again, I don't know the man.

As if he's reading my mind, Cash takes the conversation in another direction. Straight on to Harrison Holloway.

"Now tell me," he says to Clayton. "Is Harrison Holloway speaking this year?"

Clayton sighs.

"How'd you figure it out?" he asks with a wry smile.

"Charlie told me he was getting the lineup together for the website but it never got updated. Still has the speakers from last year. And I heard some murmurings that he's been doing some 'serious research,'" Cash says. "Holloway, I mean."

"I found out by running into him in town a couple of days ago," Clayton says then rubs his face. "Old bastard is same as he's always been. Arrogant."

"You think he's really been up to legitimate research?" Cash asks. His tone is skeptical, a change for him.

"They say a leopard don't change its spots," Clayton says. "Or at least my grandpa said that."

"I'm inclined to agree," Cash says. "What the hell is Charlie thinking?"

"He ain't," Clayton says. "He's soft on old Harrison because they go way back. He's not thinking with his head, he's thinking with his heart. And you know how Harrison had the entire community fooled there for a while. I imagine he's an expert at snowing on the individual level, too."

"I've never gotten close enough to find out," Cash says. "You know, he's never liked me since I interned for Blair's dad."

My eyebrow quirks up and I look at Cash. I bite back the urge to tell him let's drop the subject. I'd still rather not get into anything that involves my dad with a couple of strangers. It's complicated enough without tiptoeing around the sensibilities of people I just met who are probably big fans of his.

"Yeah," Cash says, reading my face. "Your dad didn't care for what Harrison pulled. He smelled a rat from the beginning and used his proverbial weight to rock the boat for old Holloway. He was one reason the hoax was exposed."

"So he knew my dad?" I ask.

Clayton gives me a funny look. I'm sure he's wondering about why Cash would have to explain anything about my father to me.

"In a roundabout way," Cash says. "He definitely called in to your dad's show a few times to give him some choice words. They weren't ever introduced to each other in person, though."

Lisa yawns. A few moments earlier I might have yawned too. But now this is on my mind. Harrison Holloway's hoax and whatever role my dad might have played in exposing him for the fraud he was.

"I think it's time for bed," she says.

Clayton and Cash nod and the four of us make quick work of cleaning up.

Then Lisa shows us to our rooms.

CHAPTER FIVE

I FOLLOW Lisa up to the second floor, and Cash follows closely behind me. We emerge into a hallway off the upstairs landing and turn to the right.

"We have two guest bedrooms. The nursery is the opposite direction. Our bedroom is on the first floor. But I think these rooms will be alright for your visit," she says as we reach the middle of the hallway. Two doors staggered from each other, going into rooms on opposite sides of the hallway, yawn wide and lights are on inside, almost like hotel rooms. I speak first.

"Thank you so much."

"Ladies first." Cash indicates that I should pick my room before him.

"I'll take this one." I point to the room on the right.

"Sounds good to me."

Cash hands me my bag, which he carried up here with his. I grab it and head for the room on the right.

The door is recessed slightly, another feature that makes the house seem ultra nice and fancy.

"They each have their own bathroom, so no worries about sharing one with him," Lisa says. I laugh and thank her again. Then she disappears back down the staircase.

Cash ducks into his room and mutters a quick goodnight. He's gone, the door shut, before I can ask him what he was thinking, taking me down here without warning me that there might be a guy who had bad blood with my dad.

Suddenly, being recognized seems not only like an annoyance, but a potential safety issue.

Jesus.

I retreat into my room and look around, frustration bubbling just under the surface. Maybe taking in the decor will help with that, but I doubt it. At any rate, they did the room up much like the rest of the house. Chic western style decor lines a shelf that houses a couple of rows of books. They mounted a coyote skull with flowers and some pieces that look very Santa Fe rest on the shelves with it. On the opposite wall is another deer, mounted proudly above a small dresser. Nightstand lamps illuminate the room in warm, white light.

It's lovely. Warm. Welcoming. Just the room you'd want to spend a few days away from home in.

I touch two or three things on the shelf, my mind

whirring with all the new information that dinner provided me.

So, my dad knew Harrison Holloway. Or knew of him, at least. And apparently played a pretty good-sized role in getting the guy exposed as a fraud. I can't imagine Harrison has forgotten that. The idea that he might recognize me because of a couple of magazine spreads my dad did with Blake and me growing up crosses my mind. It's not outside the realm of possibility.

People have recognized me before. Even by people that didn't know Graham Graves personally.

What do I say to the guy?

Somehow, sorry my dad ruined your career, but good luck on your new research just doesn't seem to cut it.

What would my dad have wanted me to say?

It's another one of those questions about him I may never have an answer to. He was so closed off. Blake and I never really knew him. He kept his emotions and his problems close to the vest. Maybe it was an effort to keep us insulated from them. But it stung, especially now that they had legally declared him dead.

There was no recourse. I couldn't call him up for advice. I had no idea what he would have wanted me to do. I didn't know him. I lived with him all my life and I didn't know him. Hell, I didn't even know Blake anymore. The last time I heard from him was when I gave him the money from the sale of dad's house. Our old house. It was a strange feeling to know there was only one person left in the world that shared your DNA, and they shared it almost exactly, and you didn't even know that person.

Not really.

It's a bit of a tragedy. But before I can chase those sad thoughts to their dark ends, I decide to get my laptop out and crawl into bed.

Time for some research.

I pull back the covers and slid into bed with my laptop. I crack it open and turn it on, logging in quickly and navigating to my Internet browser in a few simple clicks. It opens. The search engine stares back at me and I watch the cursor blink. I type.

Harrison Holloway hoax

Then I hit enter. The results pop up and there are so many more of them than I thought there would be. I click the first link. It's an article on a site I don't recognize, but the name makes me feel like someone like Cash would know what it was. CryptidGazette.com.

The Holloway Hoax—Well, folks. It's come to our attention here at the Cryptid Gazette that the video posted by Harrison Holloway, originally on message boards affiliated with the Bigfoot Regional Research Society, is a hoax. It probably comes as no surprise to some, as hoaxing is something that happens regrettably often within the community. Others, though, were taken in by Holloway's video and still stand by its authenticity even after famed radio host Graham Graves had a film expert and a zoologist analyze the footage. We here at the Cryptid Gazette are always skeptical of such footage when it pops up. However, Holloway's was compelling. Probably the most compelling bit of film evidence since the Patterson-Gimlin film. But thanks to the due diligence of Graham Graves, we have exposed another hoaxer to the community.

"I feel it's my responsibility to look into these things," Graves said in an interview last week with the Bigfoot Regional Research Society. "I don't like the idea of folks being taken advantage of, especially not for money, and anyone suspected of a hoax with nothing to hide has nothing to fear. Which explains why Harrison Holloway was so against having the footage examined."

I stare at the screen. I stare at my father's words.

It's so strange to see them. To know that he felt so strongly about this and that he worked so hard to expose Holloway as a hoaxer. He never so much as mentioned it to Blake or me.

The year of the article is 2006. We would have just been out of high school. Getting ready for college. And all of this was going on in our father's life and we had no clue.

I want to yell at him. Cuss him out.

It's embarrassing that strangers seem to have known him better than I did. Even Cash has a better handle on who the man was.

It's a depressing thought. One that I'd rather not follow down the rabbit hole. Not here, in a strange place, late at night. And with a shoddy cell signal to boot. There's probably only a slim chance that my texts would go through to Noelle.

Besides, I don't feel like getting so worked up over it I need to talk to someone. In a lot of ways, I guess I'm just like my dad. Vulnerability is hard for me. Asking for help is hard for me. Letting anyone get remotely close is hard for me.

Maybe all of that was hard for him, too.

I wonder if that's because he lost mom.

But that's another rabbit hole for another day. Best thought about in broad daylight. Not here in this strange bed, infinite night pouring in through the windows.

I glance outside and realize I can't see anything. But I imagine the lamp light is illuminating me perfectly for whoever might spot me.

Even though the house is so far from the road, and covered by trees, it makes me wonder if there could be someone out there watching me. I wouldn't be able to tell.

The thought makes me turn off both of the lamps. I stand up and go to the window and shut the blinds.

Just in case.

I crawl under the covers and snuggle into them. I pull the fur throw that rests on the bottom half of the bed up so that it's covering the upper half of my body. I dig my fingers into the lush surface and press it to my face, wanting comfort.

A confrontation with Cash about knowing this guy might be down here can wait until tomorrow. My anger is settling down. Not as intense as it was when he disappeared into his own room.

And maybe that's why he disappeared.

He knew I would want to confront him about it, and he probably didn't want to deal with it.

That thought reignites the fire, making me irritated all over again.

What the hell was he thinking?

CHAPTER SIX

I WAKE up before sunrise and I forget where I am for a moment.

It's still dark outside, not even a little bit of light to turn the sky dark blue. It's black, the night lingering on into the day as it does during the winter months. I get up and check just to make sure, pulling the blinds open for a moment. I look at the clock on the nightstand. Almost 7:00 am.

I look around the room, getting my bearings.

The trip with Cash. Dinner last night with Clayton and Lisa, and finally, my research about Harrison Holloway. It all comes back to me. I must have been sleeping deeply.

I wonder if the lack of city soundscape had anything to do with that. There is something a little magical about being out in the woods, spending the weekend. Even if—*especially* if—you're doing it in a luxury home.

I quickly realized the bathroom was better than any of mine at home. And this is a guest room. The shower is a walk-in and the sink is raised above the counter, a pretty orange marble. I go in there and brush my teeth, wash my face, and make short work of a shower. I get out and dry my hair, not wanting to go out in the frigid cold with a wet head, even if the idea that you'll catch a cold from a wet head is an old wive's tale. Still, it makes me think of my dad.

I hear Cash beginning to stir in his room across the hallway.

The sounds of someone getting up, padding to the bathroom, and the sound of the shower faucet being turned on are my only soundtrack as I finish getting ready.

Tonight is the first night of the festival. Apparently there will be a bonfire and a potluck dinner, at least that's what last year's event description said. I'm guessing it's the same each year. A tradition. And part of me is hoping I'll get to hear some spooky stories by the fire. Or at least get some s'mores. I'm not sure either will happen for certain and I temper my expectations.

I'm not sure how Cash is planning to spend the majority of our time today. I only know that I'll be tagging along for whatever it is.

When I leave my room, Cash is coming out at the

same time. A reminder of how unfair it is that it takes men way less time to get ready.

"Good morning," he mutters, sounding like it's anything but good.

"Didn't sleep well?" I ask him. My tone is way more chipper. He grunts and heads for the staircase.

"Too many beers?" I tease, even though he and Clayton only had a couple. "Maybe your age is catching up with you," I add for good measure.

"I'm great," he says as he heads down the staircase, but his tone is that of someone who really doesn't like early mornings. But I'm assuming Cash probably feels much the same way I do. It's impolite to sleep in when you're staying in someone else's house. I wouldn't feel comfortable with my hosts being up and around while I laze about in a guest room. Besides, if anyone has any reason to be grumpy this morning, it's probably me after the little bomb got dropped that my dad knew Harrison Holloway and they weren't exactly on good terms.

It's too early to ask Cash about that, though. And I'd rather pose the question when we get a moment to ourselves.

I follow him down the stairs and when we get into the kitchen, Clayton and Lisa are already there. Lisa sits, looking at her phone, as Clayton works on something that smells heavenly in the kitchen.

"Good morning," she says cheerily, looking up to greet both of us. Her eyes are bright, sparkling. I can tell she's a morning person. I wish I could say the same for the two of us, Cash and me.

"Morning," Cash mumbles and heads straight for the coffee machine.

"Grab me one, too, please," I say after him. He makes a grunting noise.

"What's for breakfast?" I ask. "It smells delicious," I add.

"Pancakes," Clayton says. "Banana pancakes. A specialty of mine," he goes on. "It's the only reason Lisa ever agreed to marry me."

I look at Lisa and she rolls her eyes. I smirk and giggle at that.

"Seriously," Clayton says. "I don't think it would have happened were it not for the banana pancakes."

"That's a bit dramatic," Lisa says with a smile. She rests her hand on her overly full stomach.

"Have you thought about names?" I ask her, making an attempt at conversation. It might be prying, but it's the best I can do on the little sleep I got last night.

"We're thinking about Preston if it's a boy, and Paisley if it's a girl," she says. "But I embrace the possibility that I may take one look at the kid and realize they're neither of those and have something entirely different come to mind."

"That's what I think is going to happen," Clayton says.

I smile at Lisa.

Cash returns to the table with coffee for both of us and sits down. He leans onto the table with both elbows, his arms wrapped around himself like it's the only thing holding him up. His face looks tired and he sips his coffee.

"What's y'all's plan for the day?" Clayton asks, probably more to Cash than to me.

Cash sits his coffee down and looks over at me.

"I was thinking I'd take Blair around town today and then later we could all go to the festival for the potluck and to hear some old timers share their stories around the campfire."

So my suspicion was correct. That was something that was done every year.

"Sounds good to me," I say.

"You guys will have a good time," Clayton says. There's a silence, and my mind drifts to the missing high school teacher. I wonder if there will be signs in town still. I imagine that just after he went missing, his face probably got plastered on every single available telephone pole.

And then there's Harrison Holloway and the possibility that we may run into him.

Somehow that's even less pleasant to think about than a missing person's case.

"First thing I want to show Blair is where you and I used to head off to look for Bigfoot," Cash says.

"Am I dressed appropriately?" I ask, genuinely

concerned. I look down at my sweatshirt and jeans. I've only got sneakers on today.

"Yeah, you'll be fine," Cash says without even bothering to look me over. I roll my eyes. "It's not that much of a hike. Just a couple of ravines," he adds, finally glancing at me with a smirk on his mouth.

Apparently the coffee is helping to bring him back to the land of the living. I think I liked him better sleepy.

I roll my eyes again, this time where he can see it. It only makes him laugh.

Clayton serves the pancakes shortly thereafter and we all dig in, enjoying the fruits of his labor. Or the carbs.

The three of them get into conversations about the old days and I find out that Clayton and Lisa did used to live in the city. Clayton and Cash would come down to Hobby Hollow from time to time to go Bigfoot hunting, though both of them were firmly in the no-kill camp.

"See, there are two trains of thought on that," Clayton says.

"Some people think you should absolutely kill a Bigfoot is you spot one, for science, you know?" Cash elaborates, finishing his friend's thought.

I nod and Clayton agrees.

"The other though is that these animals are already rare, possibly endangered, and shooting one does them–and us–no good," Clayton says.

"You're forgetting the woo," Lisa interjects.

"Oh, Christ. Those people," Clayton groans. "How could I forget?"

"What's the woo?" I venture, though I'm not sure I'm going to like the answer. Clayton seems annoyed just thinking about them.

"Those are the people that tell you they saw Bigfoot. In Vegas. Wearing an Elvis costume. In their motel room after he got out of his spaceship," Clayton says, scorn in his voice.

"Basically, they're people who think Bigfoot has cloaking abilities or comes from outer space," Cash says.

"Cloaking abilities?" I ask, raising an eyebrow. "Like he can camouflage himself by turning invisible," Clayton says. "Like in the movie Predator."

My eyebrows must go up another inch.

"They're a small portion of the community," Cash assures me. "Not taken very seriously and kind of frowned upon because they make it hard for people out there who are looking for a very real biological creature."

"So they give the rest of you guys a bad name?" I ask, fighting back a smirk.

"You could put it that way," Clayton says.

I nod, realizing just how deep this subculture goes. There's so much about it that I don't know at all. The intricacies are fascinating. The different groups of people based on their beliefs about the creature. It's fun.

"So have you ever seen one?" I ask Clayton.

"Sure," Clayton says. "Several times."

"What's it like?" I ask.

"Absolutely terrifying," he says.

The three of us go silent, waiting on him to elaborate.

"One time–the first time–I was standing in the woods. I was with Cash. He was a little bit further back and I looked up ahead of us. Then out of nowhere, something moved in the trees. I saw its conical head, just like they describe on the shows. I could see the sunlight shining off of its fur. It was covered head to toe. And as soon as I saw it, I just felt this sense of smallness. I knew the thing could kill me in a heartbeat if it wanted to. But it didn't seem to want to," he concluded. "It was terrifying," he reiterated. "But beautiful."

I swallow, listening to him. The account is chilling. The idea that you might see something that you shouldn't be seeing freaks me out. It reminds me too much of what just happened in my house not a month ago.

"What about you?" I ask Cash. But before I can get an answer, he springs up from the table and heads to the kitchen with his plate. And everyone follows suit.

CHAPTER SEVEN

BY THE TIME breakfast is cleaned up and everyone comes back to the kitchen table, the moment is gone and I make a mental note to ask Cash later about if he's ever seen a Bigfoot.

The morning moves slow; we pass it with conversation and Cash and Clayton reminisce about times gone by. Lisa and I talk about books. Both of us are big readers. She shows me some of her favorites and I even spot a few of mine on her shelves.

Finally, around ten, Cash breaks it up.

"Blair, you ready to go?" he asks. He catches me off guard. I wasn't expecting it somehow, deep in conversation with Lisa about how movie producers butchered her favorite book.

"Oh," I say, breaking away from the conversation. "I guess so," I tell him and then get up from my seat, offering Lisa a smile.

"You guys have fun and we'll see you tonight," Lisa says.

"Yeah, don't get lost," Clayton adds, teasing Cash.

"We won't," he says.

"We better not," I say under my breath to Lisa. She laughs and then Cash heads for the door and I follow closely behind.

He hits the door, and then we're outside, headed for his truck. Cash is bundled up in a bomber jacket that he must have brought with him. Jeans and boots complete his outfit. I'm wearing sneakers and I need to ask him about that.

"Are these sufficient?" I ask once we're inside the vehicle, kicking my foot up onto the dash for a moment.

"Please don't do that," he says, annoyed. I smirk. "And yes, those should be sufficient where we're going."

"Where are we going?" I ask as I buckle my seatbelt.

"To a place where Clayton and I used to go check for Bigfoot," he tells me with a grin and then slides his shades on.

"Have any luck with it?" I ask, wanting to probe him a little for any personal experiences he might have had with the creature. Or the alien. Except judging by Cash's assessment of the woo and how he agreed with Clayton about them, he's not a fan of that theory.

And I'm a little relieved.

Going out here, I kind of thought that was most of

the Bigfoot community. Sometimes it's nice to be contradicted.

"Well, it's where we were before Clayton saw one for the first time," Cash says.

"Have you ever seen one?" I ask him. He shakes his head.

"Unfortunately, no," he says. I can tell he really means the unfortunately part.

"It would have to be terrifying, right?" I ask. Cash heads for the road and turns out.

"Probably no more terrifying than seeing a ghost when you don't believe in them," he says pointedly.

"Somehow I think it would be worse," I tell him. "Ghosts can't really hurt you," I say.

Cash is ominously silent.

"Can they?" I ask.

"Well, some of them can. And I hate to tell you this but the spirits in your house were some of the most docile I've dealt with in years."

"Oh, gee," I say. "That's comforting."

"I guess you're coming around on that, aren't you?" he asks me without daring to take his eyes off the road.

"I guess so," I say, slightly bristled at the question. Cash knows it's a tender subject. Believing in the paranormal changes the entire sick dynamic with my memories of my father. I always thought he was full of it. That he didn't really believe in that stuff. But when Cash came to help me with my haunting, he assured me that Graham Graves really believed in the supernatural. It sort of changed the way I was looking at my father. And it made me question the way I had treated him when he was still around.

It was a prickly issue to say the least. But I was coming around. I knew what I'd experienced in the Solomon House, now my house. And it was definitely outside of anything natural I'd ever experienced. Why was it such a stretch to think Bigfoot could be out there?

I go on with the line of conversation before Cash can say anything.

"I just think seeing a flesh and blood creature you're completely unable to reconcile with any known animal might be a little rough on your psyche," I tell him.

"There are a lot of people that have come in close contact with Bigfoot that would absolutely agree with you," he says.

"That has to be life changing," I murmur.

Suddenly I'm wondering if I don't want to have my own Bigfoot experience. Maybe I do.

Cash is silent for a little while and I follow suit. But shortly thereafter, he breaks the silence.

After we've driven a little further out of town than Cash and Lisa's place is. He turns off on a gravel road.

"We're almost there," he tells me.

With as rough as the road is, I hope he's right.

We come to an area that looks like an unofficial campground that gives me some weird vibes. It looks like the kind of place you'd never go as a woman on your own. It's abandoned, despite that, it gives me the creeps.

Cash pulls in onto a piece of grass that's obviously had many cars parked over it throughout the years. He puts the truck in park and we get out. I look around at the massive trees. Here, inside the forest, there's little light penetrating the evergreens. Sifted light makes its way through the barren branches of deciduous trees.

I put on my sunglasses and go around to the front of the truck where Cash is standing.

"We'll head through the woods on that trail," he says, pointing to a little opening in the trees. I look over at it. It seems tiny. Like we'll disappear as soon as the foliage swallows us up.

I glance over at him, as if for reassurance. I'm not entirely certain I want to spend the afternoon following him through the woods. It brings me back to my question when we first set out for Hobby Hollow: exactly how much time are we going to spend in the woods and how deep are we going to go?

Now seems like an opportune time to ask, but before I can, Cash disappears into the trees, tucking his cell phone into his back pocket as he goes. It makes me wonder if he has any backup plan if we get lost.

Maybe it's just the city slicker in me, but this seems unsafe. And maybe that's the tragedy of living in a city: thinking that the rural parts of your country are terrifying. Having a genuine disconnect with nature itself, not knowing how to provide for yourself out there, and not knowing how to get back if you were lost.

All of that speaks to how much we fear nature. We think the cities are safe. But they might be even more dangerous.

I take a deep breath and follow Cash into the woods. Immediately, just as I thought I would be, I'm swallowed by foliage.

The trail is worn but not to where it makes me think a lot of people spend much time out here.

"Is this a secret spot?" I ask between breaths as Cash picks up the pace, his long legs making more progress than my short ones can keep up with.

"Not really secret," he says. "Just lesser known," he adds. "This is where Clayton and I would come and camp before we graduated from high school."

I take in our surroundings, wondering where there might be any place to camp. Only the trail is worn. The foliage on either side is pure wilderness.

"There it is," Cash says after a moment of traipsing through the woods. I come up behind him as he stops, looking off to the right. There's a tree with a white ribbon tied to it. It looks worse of the wear and like it might crumble if you laid a finger on it. "We marked the tree," Cash says with a proud smile. "Although, years ago, the ribbon was red."

I nod and look at the dense brush beyond the ribbon. It looks like no one has traveled that path in a long time.

"This way," Cash says, and he crashes through branches, trees, and bushes, much like a Bigfoot himself. I reluctantly follow, stepping over the branches on the ground gingerly. Still, I crunch several of them with each step.

I follow Cash, deeper through the winding path that seems almost nonexistent. I have panicked thoughts about what might happen if we can't find our way back. And I know it'll just piss him off if I make a comment about it. Best to keep it to myself for now.

And really, we're not that far from the truck, are we?

Finally, Cash and I both emerge from the woods onto a ridge that overlooks a valley full of trees. There's ample space, enough for a tent with a good amount of legroom.

"Is this where you camped?" I ask, feeling slightly out of breath. I try to not breathe too hard but it makes me feel like my chest is going to explode, so finally, I gulp down a few breaths of fresh air.

Cash seems unfazed by our little hike. It's a pleasant reminder to me I need to get out more. And I probably need to spend less time in front of my television and more time making my little legs carry me places.

I look at Cash after waiting for a reply for a few seconds. I see him kneeling over by some rocks on the ridge.

"What is it?" I ask him.

When he stands up and turns, he holds something in his hand. A lanyard with something dangling.

An ID card it looks like.

I walk over, and he lays it in my hand.

It's Michael Berkley's school ID.

CHAPTER EIGHT

I STARE at the laminated identification badge in my hand.

After I'm fully in tune with the reality that it actually is Michael Berkley's ID, I hand it back to Cash. He has a concerned look on his face.

"Why would that be up here?" I ask.

Cash says nothing.

"Does Clayton still come out here?" I ask him. My heart speeds up a little.

Clayton acted like they weren't close, he and Michael. That he was just an employee. Could they have gone camping together up here?

Cash walks back over to the spot where he found the ID, and I follow him. I cast a look around, trying to spot anything else. And then something catches my eye.

Red, poking out from overgrown grass. I grab it. As

I pull it from the dirt and grass and fallen branches, I realize it's faded and warped by the weather. I'm not even sure if it will open. I look at the front.

Hobby Hollow High School

It's the current school planner. I crack it open, but the pages are stuck, almost melted together from the time spent out in the elements.

"I think this might be his, too," I say, handing it to Cash.

He attempts to open it and realizes that will not happen.

He tucks the ID and the planner into his back pocket, the one not containing his cell phone.

"I think you're right," he says. Then he walks around the clearing on the ridge for a moment. He rests a hand on a tree and stares at the valley. I wonder what's going through his mind. If he's wondering the same things I am about why Michael Berkley might have been out here. "No one else ever came up here," Cash says. Almost to himself, under his breath practically.

"I guess they could," he says.

"Of course they could," I offer. "The ribbon."

He seems to think about this and finds it an acceptable piece of logic. He nods.

"It's a small town. Word of a place like this gets around. Maybe Michael came up here to think. To get away from everyone. Maybe he was dealing with some sort of stressful life event," Cash says.

"Do you think..." I pose the question. What I want to ask Cash is if Clayton showed him the place. But the question that would follow that is whether Clayton was up here when Michael left his things behind. Cash gives me a dark look.

It's a warning.

He doesn't want me to voice what I want to say. I simply nod, understanding.

And then Cash leads us back through the woods.

We get into the car. Neither of us speaks. The weight of what we haven't said hangs between us as Cash takes us back down the gravel road that leads to the main road through town.

Several things run through my mind. Going back to Clayton and Lisa's house, Cash is going to have to show him what he found. But what if he doesn't? What about how Cash looked at me? Does he think Clayton knows something? And if he does, is he willing to cover up for his friend?

All of it turns my gut in a knot.

I know that what we need to do is head to the sheriff's department headquarters with the ID and the planner. And I feel a sense of mounting relief when I realize Cash isn't headed back to Clayton and Lisa's house. He's headed into town. I breathe a deep sigh of relief.

"Where are we headed?" I ask him.

"I thought I'd show you where the festival was taking place," Cash says.

"Oh," I say, a little surprised.

It's getting weird at this point. Neither of us has spoken out loud that we need to take those things to the sheriff's department.

Finally, I can't take it.

"Don't you think we need to show those to someone?" I ask him. He seems to bristle at that. I know what's going on in his head. He's worried.

"Cash," I say. "Clayton had nothing to do with it." I pause, gauging his reaction. He makes a non-committal noise. "Cash," I say, more seriously. "You don't think he knows about those, do you?"

"Of course not," he says, but it comes out defensive and, like Cash isn't sure at all.

"We should take that to the police," I tell him.

"I know," he says, losing patience with me.

"Look–" I start. But he cuts me off.

"I'm going to take it to the police," he says. "I promise. But I want to ask Clayton about it first. If he took Michael up there, I'm sure there's a perfectly good explanation," he says. There's doubt in his voice, though. "I just want him to have a heads up."

To get his story straight.

I don't like that. Not at all.

I think back to Cash telling me I must have been the straight arrow of the family. That it surprised him. That he didn't peg me that way. How much more of a goody two shoes straight arrow could I be about this? Clayton is a perfectly nice guy. I don't know him that well, but Cash does. And if Cash trusts that there's a perfectly good explanation for why that stuff was up there, then it's good enough for me.

Except that doubt in his voice.

As he keeps driving, that niggles at me. Finally, I force it down, swallowing it for my comfort. I try to ignore it. At least for now.

If Cash doesn't do something about it in a couple of days, I'll tell him he has to.

And if he won't, I will.

With that resolved in my mind, I feel better.

And finally, Cash drives into town. It's one of those places that you can blink and miss. There's a pizza place, a gas station, a hair salon, and that's it. A few other businesses dot the road, but the place is absolutely tiny. It's shockingly so, considering that I've lived my entire life in the city. It's hard to even fathom what life might be like in a town this tiny.

I wonder if that's a good thing or a bad thing, that I can't imagine it.

But then I think about being in the woods back there and how panicked I got at even the thought that we could get lost. Maybe I'm better off in the city.

Still, it makes for a nice vacation.

Finally, we approach a church, and Cash slows down.

I'm pretty sure it's the only one in town. A nondenominational church, at that. Which surprises me slightly. We are in the middle of the Bible Belt and typically I think of small towns as having a very strict bent on which protestant sect they follow. But maybe Hobby Hollow is different. It is the Bigfoot capital of Oklahoma, after all.

Cash turns in and pulls us up in front of the church. There are people meandering in and out, obviously not churchgoers since it's the middle of a weekday.

"They're all prepping for tonight," he tells me.

"The potluck?" I ask.

"Just pray that old Betty from the salon doesn't show up with her meat surprise casserole," he says, looking over at me from behind his sunglasses. "Other than that, it's a feast to enjoy."

"Well, we can't all be bestowed with all of God's gifts," I say. Cash chuckles.

"Like you?" Cash teases.

"More like you, asshole," I say good-naturedly.

We sit in the truck for a moment, watching everyone.

"Where do they do the campfire?" I ask, glancing around and trying to see where that might be. But I don't spot a place that seems appropriate.

"It's out there," he points toward the back of the building and I spot something I didn't see immediately. An archway that seems to lead to a campground. There's lettering on top of it. Community Christian

Church Campground. 4 C's. I assume that there's plenty of space back there for a campfire.

"I see," I say to Cash.

"What do you say we go get something to eat?" Cash asks.

"I never turn down a meal," I tell him. And I am eager to see more of Hobby Hollow, if his intention is to grab something to eat in town.

"I know just the place," he says, and we head out.

CHAPTER NINE

IN THE BLINK OF AN EYE, we're in another parking lot. This time, the lot of a diner that's tucked away from the road. I didn't spot it on our first trip through town. Maybelline's. The sign is lit up in neon pink, the 's' flickering as if it's on its last leg.

Cash and I get out of the truck and head inside. The interior is much like any roadside diner you might stop at on a cross-country trip through America. The only thing that makes it unique is the fact that in every space there's a Bigfoot figurine, Bigfoot footprint cast, Bigfoot key chain, Bigfoot sticker, or other Bigfoot paraphernalia. They certainly know how capitalism works around these parts.

I run a hand over the line of key chains hanging on a rack, making them dance and jingle aloud. A woman comes walking up to us, her attention on Cash. I can hardly blame her. The guy is over six and a half feet tall. He sticks out like a sore thumb virtually anywhere he goes. It probably doesn't hurt that he's handsome, either. I would imagine his height and good looks have opened more than a few doors for him over the years. Not that I mind. Especially not since he's holding the door open behind him for me to pass through, too.

"Well, good afternoon, you two," the woman says, more to Cash than to both of us. She's in her early fifties, with raven hair that's graying at the temples. Silver strands course through her mane, giving her a wise look. "I'm Maybelline," she says.

"Nice to meet you, Maybelline," Cash offers his hand congenially. She takes it, though instead of a handshake, she holds it out for him to kiss. I snicker. "Oh, umm—" Cash fumbles for his words and then finally complies with her obvious wish. She blushes, happy with the close contact. I look away, thinking of all the ways I'll rib Cash about this soon.

"Table for two?" she asks.

"Yes," I say, looking back at the pair of them. Her eyes light on me for the first time and for the briefest moment, I catch something akin to jealousy. Irritation that I'm with Cash. And it gives me a swell of pride. It's shameful, really. I shouldn't feel that way at all. And it stirs something funny in my stomach, realizing that despite how much I shouldn't feel that way, I do.

I brush the thought away, ready to focus on more pressing matters, like what my next meal will be.

Maybelline shows us to a booth and places our menus in front of us, Cash's much more gently than mine.

"I can't help but notice that our waitress seems to be sweet on you," I tell him as I take my menu up to look it over.

"Gee," he says. "Y'think?"

I chuckle again to myself, knowing that the situation is making Cash slightly uncomfortable. It's rare that I've seen him thrown off his game. And somehow a husband-hunting cougar has done just that.

"I'm having a club sandwich," he declares.

"I'm having waffles," I tell him, putting my menu down.

Maybelline comes shortly and takes our orders, then she makes a point of asking if our checks will be together or separate.

"Together," Cash sputters quickly. I give her a sweet smile. She doesn't return it.

"I think she hopes you're going to stay here in Hobby Hollow," I tease him, sipping my water.

"Well, she can hope again," Cash says, sitting stiffly in his side of the booth. "I guess she wasn't here the last time I made a stop," he tells me. Then he casts a furtive glance around the room, presumably because he imagines her crouched somewhere, watching him.

"She's not looking at you," I say. "Sit up like an adult." He shoots me a glare but does as I say.

"The food is good, at any rate," he says, as if justifying his choice to stop by, not to me but to himself.

"I'm sure it is," I say. But Cash doesn't do much more to make conversation, and after he finishes his club sandwich in approximately three bites, he heads for the restroom. I imagine he's hiding.

I resign myself to taking the rest of my meal in solitude and glance around. There are several tables occupied by men in overalls and jeans, all talking loudly and laughing. It seems like the kind of place that probably everyone in town loves.

Just as that's what I'm thinking, Maybelline seats two customers in the booth behind ours. My back is to them.

"Good to see you, Otis," she says to one guy. "And you too, Howard," she offers the other one.

"Likewise, Miss Maybelline," one guy says. I'm not sure who's who. But with nothing better to focus on for the rest of my meal, I decide I'll just listen to them.

I cast a glance over at the bathroom and realize Cash either snuck out stealthily or he's still hiding in there. And when a man comes up and tries to open the door—and fails—I assume the latter.

My mind wanders as the guys behind me talk about fields and crops and cows. Not that those things aren't a noble pursuit, it's just that I know nothing about them and feel better left to be entertained by my own paranoid thoughts. I think about the planner and the lanyard with Michael Berkley's ID on it. And more concerning than finding it is how Cash reacted. Like he already suspected that Clayton knew those were out there. But Cash couldn't have known they were there. He wouldn't have taken me there. Why would he assume Clayton had to know those were there? And more concerning than that, why was Cash so defensive about it? It made me wonder what all I really didn't know about Clayton or their relationship to each other.

Part of me wants to badger Cash about it. But I don't even know him that well, either. We've only been friends since he offered his help in the Solomon House. The only context I've ever really seen him in has to do with the paranormal. Well, that and his dad. And Cash seems to love and care about his dad. Greatly. Perhaps to a fault.

Cash wouldn't cover up a crime for Clayton, would he? I think about how much he's willing to do for his dad. That's how he loves. He takes care of the people closest to him, no matter the cost. And that makes a dreadful feeling sink into my gut.

But before I can get any darker with it, I hear something from the booth behind ours that catches my attention.

"That's what old Holloway is saying, and so is old Karen Dunham."

"That's absurd," the other voice says. "You'd really listen to that old hack?"

"He's speaking at the festival this year, ain't he?" I can almost hear the other guy's eyes roll back in his head. It makes me chuckle to myself. "I'm just saying, stranger things have happened and I think you should hear what they have to say about it," the other guy prods his friend.

"Hell, he's saying that Bigfoot came and got Michael Berkley," the more down to earth one of the pair says.

"I'm just saying you should hear it from his mouth directly. It's not as crazy as you're thinking."

"Why on God's green earth would Bigfoot abduct Michael?"

"You'll have to ask Holloway," the other guy says.

Well, I hadn't counted on that as being one theory surrounding Michael Berkley's disappearance. But here we were. I looked again at the bathroom as I finished up my last bite of waffles. Then I grabbed my phone. There was a message from Cash. Apparently, the signal in town was slightly better than that out at Clayton and Lisa's place.

Tell me when the coast is clear

I smile at my phone and pay Maybelline, then I grab my bag and head for the door where I wait outside for Cash. I send him a text to let him know he won't be accosted on his way out.

I stand there for a moment outside, looking around at the surrounding town. It's quaint and beautiful at the same time. The sheer amount of nature that's part of its very fabric is overwhelming. Hard to imagine when you're used to living in the city. Could people out here really fall for that nonsense that Bigfoot abducted Michael Berkley? There's no way that

Harrison Holloway believed that. It sounded for all the world like a cash grab if I'd ever heard one. Or at least a cry for attention. I was ready to get Cash's take on it.

Just about then, he slinks out of the diner.

"Let's go!" he hisses, looking a bit like a cornered animal. He darts for his side of the truck. "Quick, before she sees what I drive."

"Don't you think she's going to be at the festival, anyway?" I ask as I climb up into the cab of the truck. A cab that I think is still too high. I close my door and Cash is already backing out.

"Maybe," he says with a groan. "I hadn't thought about that."

I smirk to myself. Then decide to tease him about it some more. "Just your luck, Cash Kelly. Not only are you getting a big outing, but you've likely lined up a girlfriend for yourself down here, too. I can hear wedding bells as we speak." I look over at him, smiling and enjoying his obvious discomfort.

"Why don't you focus your attention on something else?" he asks, but there's a smirk playing on his lips.

CHAPTER TEN

WE HEAD BACK to Clayton and Lisa's, Cash at the wheel. I tease him a little more on the drive back, but go easy on him when I can tell it's getting old. The last thing I want to do is make him mad at me. There's a part of me that still wants to ask him about the stuff we found in the woods. But I can tell Cash isn't comfortable talking about it.

That's the part that bothers me the most. It makes me think that there's something he isn't telling me. And I'm not sure how eager I am to find out why that is.

Part of me wants to know, and as we pull into Clayton and Lisa's drive, I can't help myself.

"Cash–" But just as we approach the house, Clayton comes outside waving his arms. I sit forward in my seat, immediately thinking that Lisa must have gone into labor. I panic, trying to think what the best course of action is when a woman goes into labor in the middle of practically nowhere. Cash rolls down his window as Clayton comes jogging up to the truck.

"You will not believe this," Clayton says, almost out of breath.

Cash throws the truck into park and throws his door open. I hop out and walk around to the other side, wondering what Clayton is talking about.

"You will not believe what I just found out," he says.

"What's going on?" Cash asks. I come up behind the two of them, wondering what's got Clayton so excited.

"Harrison Holloway is presenting something crazy at the festival. Word just leaked out from the higher ups," he says.

"Let me guess," I say.

The two of them turn around to face me. The looks on both of their faces tell me they weren't expecting this.

"This has to do with Michael Berkley's disappearance," I say.

Clayton looks at Cash, incredulous at how I knew.

"I was going to bring it up in the truck," I tell Cash as we head inside. "I overheard those guys that were seated behind us in the diner talking about it." Clayton closes the door behind the three of us.

"Well," Clayton says. "Did they mention that Karen Dunham thinks she saw something that night?"

"Was she out at the farm?" Cash asks.

I wonder when he's going to bring up the lanyard and the planner to Clayton. I also wonder if he's going to do it in front of me.

Clayton looks around, rubbing the back of his neck.

I file it away in my mind as a piece of evidence that makes me wonder what he has to hide.

Jesus. I hope Cash brings that shit up sooner rather than later. And I hope there's absolutely nothing to it. I don't want this weekend to end up being more than I bargained for, but it certainly seems like it's turning out that way.

"She'd have had to have been," Clayton says. "She's claiming she saw Bigfoot take Michael Berkley."

"So, was she out there that night?" I ask Clayton.

"I guess so," he says. Cash looks at him, eying his friend. I wonder what's going through both of their minds. I wonder what they're thinking, what Clayton might be hiding. And how far Cash will go to keep his friend safe. It only makes me more eager to find out if Cash will really go through with his promise to talk to Clayton about the things we found up on the ridge. Surely to God he will.

"Do you think she really saw something?" I ask.

"Who fucking knows?" Clayton says dismissively. "The woman's a wino. There's no telling if you can trust what she saw."

Cash glances at me, and I catch him. I wonder if he knows what's going through my mind. If he knows that I want him to ask Clayton about the lanyard and the planner right now. I want to hear it. But I'm not sure I'm going to be granted my wish. Cash probably wants to ask Clayton about that in private. And I don't blame him. I would probably do the same thing.

Suddenly, I think of Noelle. And if she was involved in something like this, I might cover for her, too.

The thought is terrifying because I know I'd do anything for Noelle. I look at Cash, waiting for what he's going to say. But he says nothing. He doesn't bring up what he found.

"So, she's not a reliable witness?" I ask, gently venturing into the conversation.

"I wouldn't think so," Clayton says. "She really is a drunk," he reiterates, this time much more calmly.

I glance over at Cash.

"What did she say?" I ask, wanting to know even if she isn't the most reliable witness. It's hard not to ask questions when someone brings up the possibility that Bigfoot might be involved in someone's disappearance.

"From what one guy helping with the festival told me, Karen saw whatever went down that night," Clayton says. "Which she claims is that Bigfoot took off with him."

"How does Holloway get involved?" Cash asks.

"Apparently Karen's been in his ear. She called him right away when the sheriff's department didn't have time for her. I'm surprised that word didn't get out about it sooner," Clayton says.

"So she wanted Holloway to investigate what she thinks she saw?" I ask.

"I guess so," Clayton confirms. "And Holloway jumped on it. So much for his real research that he's been doing."

Cash seems to think about this.

"At any rate, let's go inside. It's about time to get ready to head down there for the potluck," Clayton says. I look at Cash, waiting for him to mention the stuff that we found, but he says nothing. Finally, I accept he will not bring it up with Clayton in front of me.

I'm a little annoyed but understand at the same time. It bothers me, though, because it makes me think Cash is worried about how Clayton will respond.

We get inside and I look around, wondering where Lisa is. I don't spot her immediately.

"Lisa's taking a shower," Clayton says. "Can you guys be ready to roll in about an hour?" he asks, looking at me and Cash.

I nod, wordless. Cash does the same.

I wonder if the weight of our discovery is keeping him silent. Or if he's thinking twice about what to do with it. The thought makes my stomach uneasy. Despite that, I head for the staircase and Cash follows behind me.

CHAPTER ELEVEN

UPSTAIRS, I spin on him and he runs right into me. I hold up a hand, bracing myself against the impact. He's solid as hell, a massive walking and talking Greek statue. My hand lands on the center of his upper abdomen. I look up.

"Sorry," he mutters, stepping back. But his eyes meet mine for a brief second. I feel a flutter of something in my stomach. There's no denying that Cash is good-looking. I push it to the back of my mind and clear my throat.

"I wanted to talk to you about something," I say, my voice lowered. A look of concern flits across his features, quickly covered up by something much more comfortable, and it seems forced. There's still a little knitting between his brows.

"What?" he asks. His voice comes out like a little boy's.

"What are you going to do about the stuff we found?" I ask. "Why didn't you ask Clayton about it?"

The questions come out more hurried than I mean for them to, making me sound concerned now. Cash doesn't answer me right away, instead, he grabs my arm and leads me into his bedroom, shutting the door behind us. Somehow this is worse than if he just told me to mind my own business. I feel like he's about to tell me something I can't unknow and I'm not sure how I feel about that. His grip is strong and after he shuts the door, he releases me. I stare at him, waiting for whatever he's about to say.

"What?" I finally ask.

"There's something you should know about Clayton," he says. The statement fills me with dread. What if I don't want to know? What if I don't want to be this involved? What if I'd just rather go home? "He's never been squeaky clean," Cash goes on.

"What do you mean?" I ask, the pitch of my voice a little higher than I'd like for it to be. Cash lowers his voice even more.

"He used to be into all kinds of shit. He ran drugs illegally before he got into the weed business. There's a good chance the money that paid for this house doesn't have much to do with medical marijuana," he says. My eyes go wide. Cash goes on. "He told me he was done with that shit," Cash says, disgusted. He clenches his jaw. "I hate that I brought you down here into this," he adds.

"It's okay," I tell him, even though I feel far from okay.

"It makes me wonder how he really paid for this house," Cash says.

"Are you saying you think he's money laundering?" I ask, shocked all over again. With each question, we seem to be digging ourselves deeper into an unpleasant potential reality.

"I'm saying I don't know," his pitch goes up a little bit now. Then he stops abruptly and shushes me. He leans over by the door, listening intently. I strain my ears to try to hear whatever he's hearing. "It's fine," Cash says finally. "I thought I heard something."

"So, what are we going to do?" I press him. Cash rubs his neck and grimaces.

"I just hate this," he says.

"Me, too," I say, even though I'm not as close to either of them as Cash is. I wonder if Lisa knows all of this. She seems so sweet.

"I think the best thing we can do is to just sit on what we have," he says. "For now. I don't intend to sit on it forever." He rubs his face. "But I do want to give Clayton a chance to explain it. Just not today."

The idea that we'll be staying in their house and keeping a secret like this makes me feel sick. It makes me feel sicker that Cash doesn't immediately feel like he can just go to Clayton and tell him what he found. That's more concerning than any of it and makes me think none of this is going to end well.

Here's to hoping.

"But while we're hoping," Cash says. "We're going to do some investigating of our own."

My eyes widen.

"What do you mean?" I ask.

"We make a pretty good team when it comes to solving mysteries, don't you think?" he asks.

I nod my head wordlessly, nervous about what he's going to ask me to do. As if he's reading my mind, he goes on.

"Nothing crazy," he says. "We're just going to poke around a little bit. Keep our eyes peeled." He nods at me encouragingly, as if he's not sure I'm on board. And I'm not entirely sure either. I know I don't have much of a choice, though. I nod, quickly and silently. And I hope that I'm not getting myself into something that's putting me in over my head. The last thing I want to happen down here is to get shot by a drug lord.

Something occurs to me, speaking of drug lords and potential enemies that people might have. Or connections, for that matter. Connections that might know something about why Michael Berkley went missing.

"Cash," I say. "Why did Clayton and Lisa leave Oklahoma City?" I ask. His eyes meet mine.

"He was, uh, asked to," Cash says.

"Asked to?!" I hiss, my voice a high-pitched whisper.

"I told you," Cash says. "He was involved with

some bad people. But we haven't got much time to talk about it right now," he adds. "We'll find some time to talk later." He grabs my arm again, though this time his grip is tender, almost doting. "I'm so sorry I put you in this position," he says. "I never meant for this to happen."

"It's okay," I tell him once again.

"I just feel so bad," he says. A smirk curves his mouth. He looks down and chuckles. "I guess if you hang out with me, trouble follows wherever I go." I smirk back at him. A warm feeling pools in my stomach with his hand on my arm. I look up and he's staring at me. His eyes dart to my mouth. I want to lean in. But as soon as the feeling is there, he breaks the spell, dropping my arm back to my side.

"You better go get ready," he tells me, a softness in his voice. I don't want to go. I want to stay in here with him. But I listen and turn for the door. Then I slip out into the hallway and head to my bedroom.

CHAPTER TWELVE

I CLOSE the door behind me and slide down the back of the door.

Dramatic? Perhaps. But the situation seems pretty dramatic.

I wish there was a way to just read Clayton's mind and know which way this was going to go. And then to be done with it. I sit there for a moment then pull myself together. It occurs to me that I might not be the best candidate for a Bonnie and Clyde type relationship.

It is true what Cash guessed about me: I'm a straight arrow.

Finally, I get myself together and get off the floor. I run my hands through my hair, trying to make it look presentable again. Our little walk into the woods left it looking a little wild.

I push the stuff about Michael Berkley and

Clayton to the back of my mind and instead, I focus on Harrison Holloway.

There's a next to nothing chance that he won't be there tonight, I think. He seems like the kind of guy that likes to make waves and making an appearance at the opening ceremonies of this thing sounds right up his alley.

But who knows? I might get lucky. And there's always the possibility that he might look at me and have no idea who I am. That would be the idea situation, as far as I'm concerned. Before I can get too deep in thought, a voice from down the hall startles me. Clayton's.

"Hey!" he hollers. I jump at the sound. Maybe it's the combination of the shock and the fact that it's his voice. I'm not sure. It's almost like I can sense that he knows we were talking about him. That's absurd. There's no way he could know that. Is there?

I take a deep breath and brace myself for opening the door. I have another absurd thought: that he'll be waiting on the other side, ready to scare me. What the hell is going on in my brain right now? I feel like in some ways I've stepped into a situation from monster movie or a thriller. This doesn't have the vibe of a Miss Marple mystery. There seem to be a lot more nefarious things going on.

I grab the door knob and throw the door open. Clayton isn't there. But Cash is.

"Oh," I say, involuntarily.

"Expecting someone else?" Cash asks. His tone is playful, a smirk on his face. But he sees almost immediately that I'm startled. "Are you okay?" he asks, changing his demeanor. He reaches for me but seems to think better of it. His hand falls at his side.

"I'm fine," I tell him. I turn and quickly gather my things: just my purse and cell phone.

"I'm ready," I say.

"Let's go then," he says, his tone becoming somewhat chipper again.

I close the door to my bedroom and head down the hallway that leads to the stairs, Cash in front of me.

And I say a little prayer that mind reading isn't really a thing.

Somehow, by the grace of God, the ride over to the church isn't awkward. Lisa fills the truck cab with conversation about the baby. Everyone engages. The topic is safe, pleasant, and passes the time on the way over there. I'm grateful to her. But I can't express that. I wonder if Lisa knows exactly why she and Clayton moved out here. I wonder if she knows anything about who he used to be. She seems to sweet. Like the knowledge of any of that darkness would absolutely destroy her.

When we turn into the church parking lot, it's an entirely different scene than the one Cash showed me. The place is absolutely crawling with people. It looks like an anthill, everyone going in and out, meandering about, carrying things to and fro. It's clear that this really is the event of the year out here. And so many people seem to have come. There are tons of out of state plates. They range from Maine to Washington and all the way to the southeastern part of the nation: Florida. This really must be the place to be when it comes to Bigfoot investigation.

I try to fathom it. A place like Oklahoma doesn't get a lot of recognition. But this event is ours, and people from all over the country seem to be flocking here. I know there are people who make fun of it. They'll think these folks are just hillbillies. And maybe they are. I don't know. But it brings my dad to mind. And he wouldn't have thought that, I don't think. From what Cash has told me about the guy, I think he might have held a gathering like this as sacred. Especially judging by the way he handled Harrison Holloway. In a strange turn of events, I feel a swell of pride at the idea that I'm Graham Graves' daughter. It feels a bit like the Twilight Zone.

"Looks like we're going to have to park out back," Clayton says. The truck bounces, shifting my innards around, when he hits a giant pothole on the road that leads us into the campgrounds. After a sharp turn to the left by some trees, we emerge into what looks like camper central. There are tons of RVs and the like.

We drive all the way down to the end and people are milling about, most of them heading up to the church building. Finally, we reach a point where trucks and cars have found parking spaces, and Clayton slides into the first free one he spots, which happens to be at the end of the line.

Jesus, this place really is packed.

He pulls all the way in and shuts off the engine.

"Well, here we are, ladies and gentlemen," he says.

In the stillness of the silent cab, I find myself transfixed by all the people moving around us. They come from all walks of life. Some of them look like they've never come out of the woods for the entirety of their existences. Others look like they've never set foot outside the city. And there's a whole bunch of them who fall somewhere in between.

My mind is racing, and a thought comes to me, somewhere out of the chaos in my brain. What would it be like if dad was here with me?

It's bittersweet, melancholy almost. And it's the first time that a thought like that has really hit me.

Sure, I've missed him. But there's always been a bitterness that accompanied that feeling. This is pure. A wondering at what he'd say. What he'd be interested in seeing. What he'd scoff at and say was entirely false. And what he'd have to offer in the way of wisdom as we left. The purity lasts a moment, but it's followed by the knowledge that my dad was so closed off, that probably couldn't have ever been a moment that existed in reality. And instead of pissing me off, it just makes me incredibly sad. And that's a new twist. Usually, I can descend into anger about him, spiraling until I need a box of wine to make it go away. But this sadness just sits on my chest, like a demon trying to keep me from breathing. It's heavy, and I'm not sure what to do to make it go away.

"You ready?" Cash asks me. He's already halfway out of the truck and I realize that Clayton and Lisa are gone. I've been sitting here in my own little world for a little too long.

"Oh," I say. "Yeah."

"Where were you?" Cash asks as we start the long trek up to the church. Clayton and Lisa have gone ahead, likely to find her somewhere to sit, if any places remain. In a moment of startling transparency and vulnerability, I tell Cash the truth.

"I was thinking about my dad," I say. "To be honest."

I glance up at him as we walk and he raises an eyebrow. In the short time that we've known each other, he's probably the one person that I've been most honest about that relationship with. Noelle knows some things, but Cash knows more.

"What were you thinking?" he asks gently. People rush past us, eager to get themselves a spot inside the church. I wonder what exactly the opening ceremonies of this thing are going to look like.

"I was just wondering what it would be like to attend something like this with him," I say. Vulnerability isn't my strong suit, but somehow this feels easy. Maybe it's the strength of the emotions I'm navigating, and a wish to be understood. Or maybe it's the person I'm telling this to.

"I imagine he'd have a few choice words when it comes time for them to reveal that old Holloway is giving a presentation," Cash says with a chuckle.

"I don't doubt that," I tell him. "I read up about it. He really went hard at that guy."

"That was something about your dad that I always admired. He was always standing up for the little guy. He didn't like the idea of anyone being taken for a ride, especially not when someone was going to profit from it."

"I guess he wasn't so bad after all," I offer Cash with a smile. It's probably the only nice thing I've ever said about my dad in Cash's presence. He gives me a surprised look, but doesn't dare comment on that fact.

Good for him. I'm not sure I'm ready to unpack everything. But I have a feeling that when I do, I'll want to do it with Cash.

He remains silent and we head up to the building. People rush past us to get to the door. And I catch some snippets of conversation. One thing particularly catches my attention.

"He said he'd be here later," one person says.

"I can't believe he's showing his face after all this time," a woman answers them.

I glance over at Cash, and judging by the look on his face, he's catching all of this, too. Harrison Holloway will be here after all.

CHAPTER THIRTEEN

WHEN WE GET INSIDE, Clayton hollers at us. There's a cacophony of sound around us. People chitter chattering away about this and that, there seems to be an air of excitement to it all. He and Lisa are standing by the wall. Apparently she didn't get a seat.

I scan the room for any that might be empty, wanting to offer it to her. Cash leads to the way over to them, parting the crowd of people like Moses parting the Red Sea.

"There you are," he says to his friend as we approach. "Lisa, do you need somewhere to sit?" Cash asks.

"I'm okay, really," she says with a smile. "Besides, after they open things up, we'll move into the camp-grounds' mess hall and there will be plenty of places to sit."

Cash nods, as if this is good enough for him.

"Heard someone mention Holloway on the way in. Says he won't be here until later," Cash says to Clayton.

"Old bastard probably wants to make an entrance. You know how much he loves attention."

It's hard to imagine that someone who perpetuated one of the biggest hoaxes in Bigfoot history wouldn't like attention. That–and money–are likely the two main driving factors as to why he did it. That explanation aside, I still have bad butterflies in my stomach at the idea that he might recognize me. I don't really want to engage.

Just as I'm thinking that, someone comes scurrying up to us. A little man with a full white beard and a get up that makes me wonder if he's a lumberjack.

"You're Blair Graves!" he declares.

My eyes widen and I want to shush him so no one else gets any wild ass ideas about coming up to me. But it's too late. Other people are starting to turn their heads.

"Yeah," I say dumbly, not able to think of anything intelligent to reply with. But he seems excited enough for the both of us. I glance at Cash for strength, but his eyes are focused on the little guy.

"I used to listen to your daddy's show religiously," the guy says. "I even have the two magazines that you were in with him!" I'd only thought about those magazines for the first time in a long time when Cash and I were about to embark on our journey. I have copies.

Many. They're somewhere in my dad's things. I cringe.

"He was a hell of a guy," the little man says to us. Just then, someone else comes walking up, and I recognize him instantly. One of the guys from the booth behind the one Cash and I ate lunch in.

"There you are," he says to the little guy. The little guy turns to his friend.

"This is Graham Graves' daughter, Billy," he says.

"Well, I'll be damned," he says to his little friend. I glance at Cash and see a smirk on his face, then decide to throw him to the wolves.

"I'm sure you guys know my companion here," I say. "Cash Kelly." They turn their attention on him and it starts all over again.

I watch as Cash graciously handles the whole interaction. He's kind and warm with them. He signs some stuff. They seem like their whole trip down here has been made. And then they turn to me and thank me for my time as well. Cash turns to me as they leave.

"Wow," Clayton says. "I didn't realize I'd be attending this thing with a couple of celebrities," he says with a smirk. I feel my cheeks heat up. I didn't realize it either.

"There's Holly!" Lisa says and she whistles at a woman walking across the other side of the room. The woman looks up and when they make eye contact, she smiles and heads on over our way. "She's a friend of mine," she leans in and tells me. Clayton and Cash start their own conversation and Holly gives Lisa a warm hug.

"I'm so glad you came!" Holly says.

"Holly, this is my new friend Blair," she introduces us. I shake Holly's hand. "Holly is a teacher at the high school," Lisa tells me.

"I'm sorry about what's been going on for you guys," I tell Holly. She smiles graciously.

"Thank you," she says. "You know, Michael was well-loved by all his students. The faculty, too," she adds. But just before we can get into too much more conversation, a woman taps on her shoulder.

"Holly," she says. And Holly turns and smiles at the woman, wrapping her in a hug.

"Linda!" she says. A younger woman is with her. A girl really. Probably not older than fifteen. She has a sullen air about herself, like any self-respecting teenager does.

"Hi, Haley," Holly says to the girl.

"Hi, Miss Grimes," Haley says back, her voice devoid of color.

"Ladies, this is my friend Lisa and her friend Blair," Holly says to the other two women. Or the woman and her daughter.

"Haley, Linda," Holly says, indicating each of them. I put out my hand and shake Linda's. She cheerfully smiles back at me as she takes my hand. When I shake Haley's, though, she gives me a limp fish, like she'd rather die than greet me. I want to tell her I get it.

After my last little interaction, I'm wanting to disappear from this place.

"Well, we're going to go find somewhere to wait," Linda says.

"Me too," Holly adds. "It was good to see you!" she tells Lisa. "And nice to meet you, Blair!" she adds to me. I wave as they disappear.

"I think Haley is a student of Holly's," Lisa tells me. The guys are still deep in their own world, probably oblivious to the interaction that just happened. "Freshman, I believe. She's mentioned her before to me. Apparently, she took Michael's disappearance hard. He was her cross country coach. And now they're scrambling to find one. I think Haley was looking at potential full rides to college before he disappeared."

"No wonder she's so sullen," I say. "I would be, too."

"Right?" Lisa asks. "He was basically her ticket out of here. And I get why kids that grew up here would want out. They want to see the outside world, you know?"

"I can totally imagine that," I tell her. I feel for Haley and say a little prayer that she finds another way out of this town.

"It's funny, isn't it?" Lisa asks.

"What?" I reply. "The teenagers here can't wait to leave. And adults from the city can't wait to get here. They come for vacations all the time in the summer.

That's how I fell in love with it. Clayton had been down here a lot. I hadn't. But once I saw it, I knew it was the right place for me."

I nod, thinking about what Cash told me about how Lisa and Clayton ended up here. Her words make me wonder just how aware she is of why they moved down here. Does she think it's just because she told him she loved the place? Or does she know everything?

I glance at Cash again, wondering if he's hearing any of this. But he's absorbed in conversation with Clayton. Before I can get too deep into my own thoughts about the whole thing, someone taps a microphone somewhere in the room. I look up at the front, at the pulpit, and a guy is standing there.

He wears blue jeans and a plaid shirt. He looks to be in his late sixties.

"Is this thing on?" he jokes. A smattering of laughter breaks through the crowd as everyone quiets down. "I guess it is," he says with a chuckle. The room falls mostly silent, a few conversations carry on until he starts speaking again. "Well, I'm Charlie, and most of you already know that," he says. "I just wanted to welcome everyone down to the Bigfoot festival here in Hobby Hollow!" A cheer rolls through the crowd, making the building shake around us.

I wonder if any of the church services ever do the same, but I doubt it.

"First things first," Charlie says. "Everyone knows the rules. No booze in the campground. No fighting."

My eyebrow arches at those. I wonder who might have been the culprit that made either of those rules necessary. I glance back at Cash and he gives me a smirk. I find myself smiling as I turn back around.

"Now," Charlie says. "As long as everyone can follow those, we should have a great time over the next few days." There's some chuckling in the crowd that makes me think that there are plenty of people that intend on breaking the no booze rule. It makes me chuckle myself. "Now, without further ado. Let's open this thing up," Charlie says. "Welcome to the thirteenth annual Bigfoot festival here in Hobby Hollow, Oklahoma. It's our claim to fame and we couldn't be more proud. A lot of people don't realize that southeastern Oklahoma has just as many Bigfoot sightings as the Pacific Northwest. And a lot of our friends from up there have decided to join us."

Several people holler that must be from the Pacific Northwest. It confirms my data gathering from the parking lot. People really do come from all over to attend this thing.

"Everyone can check out the schedule for speakers," Charlie says. "It's posted in the atrium. Now everyone have fun, and let's go have some food and hear some stories later."

As he steps down from the mic, thunderous applause fills the church. I look back at Cash and wonder what, exactly, I'm in for here.

CHAPTER FOURTEEN

LIKE SHEEP BEING HERDED, everyone heads for the atrium at once, hellbent on getting to the campground meal hall. The four of us hang back, not keen on getting swept up in the crowd with Lisa eight months pregnant. Instead, we watch as people pass and I take another opportunity to wonder at the diversity of the crowd.

It really is amazing how many people this festival draws down here. I'm not sure I've even heard of Hobby Hollow at any point in my life before this.

We stand there, hanging back for several minutes. About ten pass and the crowd seems to thin, most people having already made their way out to the meal hall. A few stragglers hang on but Cash, Lisa, Clayton, and myself are the last people out of the building. And I haven't seen Holloway, just as predicted.

Clayton and Lisa walk ahead of us and Lisa takes

her husband's hand. I fold my arms over my chest, trying to stay the bitter bite of the wind. It's excruciatingly cold now as the sun begins to set.

"You need another jacket?" Cash asks.

"I'm fine," I tell him. I'm wearing one that's probably too thin for the elements. But I'd never had the opportunity to test it so I couldn't be sure when I packed it. But yep, it's way too thin.

"I brought an extra one," Cash says. I give him a funny look. "I saw you leaving in that and knew you'd need something else," he says with a smirk. "Come on." He tells Clayton and Lisa that we're headed back to the truck for a jacket switch. Clayton nods and he and Lisa continue on toward the meal hall. I follow Cash to the back of the lot where we parked.

"Why didn't you just tell me this wouldn't work?" I ask him as we near the truck. Cash shrugs his shoulders and turns away from me for a moment, looking back at the people filing into the large outer building on the campgrounds. I smile to myself.

I hate that, like a teenager, I'm excited he's giving me a jacket of his. But here we are.

Maybe I need to get out more.

Cash opens the backseat of the truck and pulls a burgundy jacket that looks fit for the elements. I shrug mine off and my sweatshirt is no match for the cold. I slip into his jacket and it swallows me. I look like a shrimp dressed in a lobster's clothes. Cash smirks at me after he tosses my jacket back into the truck.

"You look cute," he says. Immediately, both of us go silent. There's something in the way he says it that makes me blush deeply. He's not just being funny. And he seems to realize the same thing. The pair of us stand there for a moment and he clears his throat.

"Uhh–"he says. "Ready to go on over there?"

"Yes," I say. "Yes." I repeat the word once more for good measure, trying to dispel any of the awkwardness between us in the moment. But as we walk towards the brightly lit meal hall, I swear I can feel Cash reaching for my hand, hidden in the sleeve of his jacket.

The raucous conversation and laughter in the meal hall all but obliterates anything that might have been happening between me and Cash. The spell is broken. And I can't decide if I'm sad about that or relieved. There's no denying that I feel the chemistry between us. And I think he does, too, certainly. But chemistry is one thing. Acting on it is another.

I try to focus back on the whole reason I'm down here. To experience this festival first hand.

In the back of my mind though are two things: where the hell is Harrison Holloway? And what happened to Michael Berkley?

It doesn't seem like the two questions should intersect, but Holloway seems to have seen to that, judging by what people are saying in the shadows.

For the first time today, I'm eager to see Holloway in person. I want to hear what he has to say about the whole thing. It'll likely be ridiculous, but the police don't seem to have anything resembling a lead at this point.

My stomach churns, thinking of the lanyard and the planner. And why they ended up in a place that was special to Clayton. I almost want to ask him myself, and rip the bandaid off. But as all of this is circulating around in my mind like a gerbil running far too fast on an exercise wheel, I get lost in the opening of the festival.

People are laughing, talking, and it's obvious that for some of them, this is the only time they get to see each other. People from far parts of the country come together for this once a year event, it seems. The hall is rustic. It's like a log cabin, but vastly larger. Long tables run from one end to the other, and a cafeteria style set up is at the front, where people grab something to eat.

Cash and I get in the back of the line, which is still stretching pretty far back, but most of the people have already gotten their food and found seating next to old friends and acquaintances.

"This is something else," I tell Cash.

"Oh, just wait," he says with a smile. I can tell he's enjoying this. Probably also enjoying that he's experiencing it all for the first time vicariously through me. "This is nothing. The campfire tales are where it's at."

I raise an eyebrow, eager to get to that part of the evening.

The line moves quickly and pretty soon Cash and I have chicken fried steak, mashed potatoes, and green beans. All of which I find to be excellent when I get a taste of them. We find Lisa and Clayton, sitting with Lisa's friend Holly.

I spot Linda and Haley Stone across from us at another long table. Haley still has the look of a tortured teenager that would rather be dead than anywhere near this group of old fogies. It makes me smirk, thinking of myself as a teenager. God, I couldn't stand going anywhere with my dad. Neither could Blake. It was like the most unhip thing that either of us could be caught doing. It sends a little pang of regret through me, straight through my heart then it bounces off my spine. I feel myself starting to get emotional. And that's the last thing I want.

"How have things been at the school since Michael disappeared?" Lisa asks Holly.

"It's been strange, you know?" Holly says after a bite of chicken fried steak. "A lot of the kids had really close relationships with Michael. Especially the ones on the cross country team. I feel for them."

"Have they given up the search?" Clayton asks. His tone is curious, but there's something else in it that makes me feel uneasy.

"For the most part, yeah," Holly says. "The police really haven't found any leads that I'm aware of. Or at least Kevin hasn't told me about any," she adds. Moments ago she revealed that her husband Kevin is one of the deputies that went out searching for Michael when he first disappeared.

"You must have all kinds of insight into this," Cash says, and my eyes widen. I look at him. Then I look at Clayton, who stares at Cash with something akin to shock.

"I guess you could say that," Holly says. "Things like this just don't happen down here, you know?" she goes on. "It's a small town. Everyone knows everyone else. So I think the scary thing is that there could be someone right here in the community that's responsible for whatever might have happened to Michael."

Clayton nods at that, seeming to be thoughtfully considering his potatoes. Lisa looks at her friend with compassion. And I glance at Cash, who glances at me.

"Hard to believe," Cash says. "I'm sure."

"It really is," Holly goes on. "I'm just worried about the kids, you know? So many of them loved Michael and looked up to him. He worked for you, didn't he Clayton?" she turns the conversation around. Clayton looks a little surprised. He glances at Lisa and then forces a smile.

"He did ," he says.

"I know some of the parents weren't keen on the idea that teachers were taking part time jobs at the farm," Lisa says. Almost like she's apologizing on Michael's behalf. Holly makes a dismissive gesture.

"People know how hard it is for teachers right now," she says. "If they don't like it, they can get over it."

It brings to mind an idea for me. That maybe

someone couldn't get over it. Maybe some super conservative religious nut. Someone who thought such a thing might corrupt the children.

"How many people live in Hobby Hollow?" I ask Holly.

"About 450," she says. Cash whistles.

The amount is tiny, narrowing the pool of suspects considerably. And it's not likely that anyone here for the Bigfoot festival can be counted among them. Not the locals. And it was likely a local who might know something about Michael Berkley's disappearance. Not a stranger.

The conversation shifts to other things, more pleasant things. Like Lisa and Clayton's baby due in only a month. Potential names. Old stories about what Clayton and Cash used to get up to when they were younger. The air seems lighter, not clouded with suspicions. At least for now.

I look around the room. I'm looking for one person in particular, but I don't see him.

Harrison Holloway.

I memorized his face from the articles I read. He's an older guy. Gray hair, no facial hair. Extremely well kept. He looks like he could be a university professor, though I guarantee he lacks the credentials. In videos I watched of him, he comes across as a snake oil salesman. It makes me even more eager to see him present. What could he possibly have to offer on the case of Michael Berkley? Is that what he's going to talk about this weekend? Surely to God not. How inappropriate could a person get? There's no telling what Holloway has up his sleeve though. From everything I could gather, he was eager to reinsert himself into the Bigfoot community and into the conversation surrounding research of the creature.

Only time would tell.

CHAPTER FIFTEEN

AFTER DINNER, people start disappearing out of the meal hall, heading for the campgrounds, I presume. And likely trying to snag a seat for the storytelling.

I'm eager to get out there, and I hope that we do get a good seat. Cash made it sound like this is one of the highlights of the weekend, and I trust him.

"Shall we?" he finally asks after people are starting to get up and around, tossing their plates into the trash.

The five of us, including Holly, head out of the meal hall onto the campgrounds. It's even colder than it was when we left the church earlier, but Cash's jacket seems to be entirely insulated from the cold, and therefore I am too. My jeans on the other hand, not so much.

"Let me get the blankets out of the truck," Clayton says as we head for the campgrounds.

"There's a little amphitheater down there where

they'll tell the stories," Cash tells me. He's excited and his enthusiasm is catching. After a quick trip to the truck, we all head out, blankets in tow. And Cash finds us some seats at the back of the amphitheater. It's a Roman knockoff, probably built in the fifties or sixties and likely used for church plays or for the Passion of the Christ in the holiday season. But tonight, it belongs to Bigfoot.

There's a fire burning in a pit down in front of the first row. The rest of us aren't quite as lucky. The further back you get, the colder it is. But the blankets Clayton gave us seem to provide ample protection. Cash sits down beside me and realizes he doesn't have one.

"We can share," I tell him. He raises an eyebrow, but quickly changes his expression. I blush and hand him part of the blanket. He scoots closer until our thighs are touching and for a moment, I don't breathe. And I'm almost positive that Cash isn't breathing either.

Charlie takes the stage and I sigh, unable to keep from it. I take a deep breath, inhaling the woody scent on the air and the smell of burning leaves.

"Well, folks. Now for the main event," Charlie says. "Without further ado, let's get our first speaker up here."

"That's Linda's nephew," Holly whispers to me on my other side. I nod, watching the burly man get up to speak. He's as tall as Cash and wearing coveralls that look like they're meant for this weather. He's twice as wide as my friend next to me and his boots are gigantic. He's the kind of guy I wouldn't want to piss off in a bar fight.

"My name is Nathan and I got a story for y'all," he says. the crowd goes silent, their attention all his. The crackle of the fire grows loud and you can hear a pin drop. I find that a chill descends both of my arms as he begins to speak, and I shiver. Cash glances at me and scoots closer. "This past December, I had me another encounter. Now y'all know that I've ran into things in the past out there in the woods. And I'm not someone that just believes anything I hear. For a long time I tried to talk myself out of some of the things I'd seen. But this one last December was one for the books.

"I was out tending to my animals and I noticed that the lock on the freezer outside my house was broken. It looked like it had been smashed. So I opened it, and all the meat I'd had in there was ravaged. It was like someone just ate it all right there on the spot. Didn't bother to take it out or cook it or anything.

"So I put another lock on it and I thought maybe it was a bear that got to it. But a few nights later, I hear something outside. I grabbed my rifle and expected to see a bear out there. But that ain't what I saw. This creature was seven feet tall. The freezer hit him mid-thigh and it hits me at the waist. He had a rock and he was banging on the lock to get into the freezer. I was standing there at the door, staring at him. Then suddenly, we locked eyes.

"This thing stared at me for a good two or three minutes. And then it threw the rock at my door and shattered the glass. Then it ran off into the forest and I took a couple of shots at it, but missed.

"That next week, I could hear them outside. each night getting closer and closer to the house. A group of them, like they were hunting me or something. There would be a howl from one direction, then a howl from another direction. Like they were triangulating. The way coyotes do.

"I never did catch sight of them after that, but that was my experience. Them things is out there, folks, and they'll tear you apart if they get half a chance."

Instead of tearing into applause, the crowd is solemnly silent after he takes his seat. They take this dead seriously. And I feel fear creeping up the back of my spine. I glance around behind us and am glad to see that there are plenty of people still standing there, listening in rows behind us. At least a Bigfoot won't sneak up on us.

"You alright?" Cash whispers. I turn around to face him, noticing that we're closer than I think we've ever been. I feel my breath hitch in my chest. I swallow.

"I'm fine," I say.

"Spooky, right?" he asks.

All I can do is nod. It is spooky, and alarming. And makes me feel like every instinct I have about being afraid of the woods has been right all along. Suddenly, I'm wishing that I'd be spending the night in my own haunted house rather than at Clayton and Lisa's. What's preventing one of those things from showing up over there?

"Do you think he's telling the truth?" I whisper to Cash.

"I think so," he says. "I think it's gospel down here. These people live in the woods. They know the woods better than anyone from the outside. And who's to say there aren't things in there that we just don't understand?" he looks at me. We lock eyes. And I think about my confession to him that if I believed in ghosts, it opened up a whole can of worms with my father. That I might have been wrong about him and the things he believed. And that if ghosts are real, what else is, too? Could this be one of those things?

The thought chills me to the bone. Another speaker gets up, and another, but none of their stories chill me the way that the first guy's did. Linda's nephew. This goes on into the night, and I begin to realize that I don't want it to end. Maybe its' the stories. Maybe it's the sense of camaraderie.

Or maybe it's the person next to me that makes this magical, his thigh pressed against mine.

CHAPTER SIXTEEN

MORE PEOPLE GET up and speak, and by the time Charlie takes the stage after the last speaker, it's well past midnight. Which I wasn't expecting. I look at my watch and my eyes widen. Just seeing the time makes me yawn, or maybe it's the fact that with Charlie taking the stage, the adrenaline that's been going through my veins during the storytelling has had a chance to calm down. Either way, the weariness of the day hits me. Cash catches me yawning and he does the same.

"Ready to call it a night?" he asks in a whisper.

"Just about," I say.

People have started to chatter as Charlie closes things up. Probably talking about their favorite stories of the night. Still, Linda Stone's nephew holds that place for me. The story was absolutely chilling. A horror story. Not some crazy person's encounter with Bigfoot.

And that's another thing I noticed. All of these people are down to earth. None of them sounded crazy as they were relaying the things they'd experienced.

But just as I'm about to tell Cash that I'm ready to go so he can see what the consensus is for our gang, Holly whispers, "Holy shit! There he is!"

I whip my head around, looking at the stage in the amphitheater. And lo' and behold, it's Harrison Holloway. As promised, fashionably late. Everyone quiets. There are a few gasps throughout the audience. And Holloway walks over to Charlie and takes the mic without warning, cutting Charlie off mid-sentence. A look of shock fleets across Charlie's features, but he tries to hide it, turning and smiling at the audience as if to say everything's okay. Clearly it's not according to Charlie's plan even though the rumors of Holloway showing up late in the evening have been circulating all day.

I glance at Cash, but his attention is glued to Holloway. Then the man begins to speak.

"Never thought I'd find myself here again," he says, somewhat joking. There's a little prickliness to the words, as if he holds some bitterness about what happened to him. Enough of it that I lean closer to Cash and try to make myself small, even though I don't think there's any way he could pick me out of a crowd.

Better safe than sorry.

Charlie stares at him, the look on his face betraying the fact that he seems to be wondering if he made a bad decision in letting Holloway show up at the festival, let alone speak. I'm eager to see the reactions when that gets revealed, though I don't know if it will tonight. But Holloway seems to be a showman, and there is a good chance he'll mention it, if only for the shock value.

"As all of you know, I was sort of let go from the Bigfoot community about fifteen years ago," he says. "Thanks to a busybody that didn't believe what he saw."

There it is, the mention of my father. I knew it was coming on some level.

"But enough of that," Holloway says. "I'm here tonight to talk to you about a very real problem that you've got right here in Hobby Hollow."

I feel Cash growing tense beside me. His arm and leg flex, and I feel the ripple of the muscle moving. I glance over at him and see that his jaw is doing the same thing, the muscles dancing below the surface of his skin as he grinds his teeth.

I wonder if that's purely because of how he feels about my dad, or if he's worried about how I'm feeling. But he doesn't break his stare away from Holloway. I imagine there are several people in the audience doing the same thing.

"I got a phone call from Karen Dunham about a

month ago," Holloway says. I already know where this is going. "Karen told me that she witnessed something. An abduction of sorts. And it just so happens that this is right around the time that Mr. Berkley went missing. Now I've been performing a lot of research on the topic and I want to share it with you." I want to groan. This can't get worse. "I want to take you all out to the place Michael Berkley was last seen and show you a reenactment of what Karen saw."

Something–some sort of chaotic energy–ripples through the crowd. There are gasps and some angry words. People begin chattering. Holloway holds up a hand to silence them.

"I just want you to hear me out on this," he says.

Someone barks out a laugh and says, "Like we did on the tape you had all those years ago?"

Though Holloway is illuminated by the orange glow of a fire, his face still flushes with anger. It's obvious that all of that is still very close to the surface for him.

"You don't have to go," he tells the man. "But for those of you that do, I think you'll find that my theory holds some water."

I was wrong.

There's going to be an reenactment of a Bigfoot abduction after midnight at Clayton's weed farm.

Things can always get worse.

I sigh and glance at Cash, who seems to have let go

of some of his anger. He looks more frustrated than anything now. Clayton stands up beside Holly and Lisa grabs his arm. I hear her hiss beside him.

"It'll just look bad if you don't let him do this," she says. I look over at them. Holly seems not to have heard, but Cash leans in and whispers in my ear.

"I want to go," he says.

"Do you think Clayton will go for that?" I ask him. I don't know that he will. I can't imagine him being very fond of watching all of this play out right outside his business.

"I've got a plan," he whispers.

The four of us walk to the truck in silence. Holly said goodbye to all of us before we left, seeming none the wiser to all the tension that both Cash and I seemed to feel with Clayton. It's obvious that he has no desire to go out there. His jaw is set in the moonlight and he looks much like Cash did a little while earlier, muscles twitching beneath his skin.

I glance over at Cash as we walk, wondering what his plan is. How's he going to get Clayton to take us out there, willingly? I can't imagine that it would go over well if we all went back to the house and then Cash and I left to go see the show.

I tell myself not worry about it as we get into the truck. Then Cash breaches the silence.

"I think we need to go over there," he says. The words are like rocks shattering glass, the tension is so thick.

"Why the hell do you think that?" Clayton asks, looking at Cash in the rearview mirror.

"You think it's a good idea to let Holloway be running around outside your property in the middle of the night unsupervised?" he asks his friend.

"He's got a point," Lisa says. Her tone is no longer the one I'm used to. The chipper, vibrant one. She seems upset and sullen. I swallow, noticing how dry my mouth is. There's no denying that I want to go see whatever show Holloway is going to put on. But a mounting sense of dread begins to creep in at the edges of this four-day weekend. The sense that the people we're spending our time with might know something about Michael Berkley's disappearance after all.

Clayton throws the truck in reverse and we head that way, toward the weed farm. A mass of red tail lights lead the way. Everyone in town seems to be going the same direction. Everyone wants to see what Holloway has to say, and I'm not sure if that's a good thing or a bad thing.

The tension comes back in the cab of the truck, thick enough to bite into. I glance over at Cash, almost looking for reassurance, I guess. Or for him to tell me that everything's okay. Or, ideally, that we'll just go home tomorrow morning. Or tonight, when we get back to the house. That would be for the best, I think.

But instead, he says nothing. And I'm left with this sinking feeling in my gut as we make our way out of town. The cars move slowly, like molasses on the winding roads with dense foliage on either side. And as I'm looking at those trees, a dark thought occurs to me.

No matter how Michael Berkley disappeared, if he ended up in those woods with someone or something he shouldn't have, there's no way it hell anyone is ever going to find him.

CHAPTER SEVENTEEN

THE TRUCKS and cars that make their way out to the weed farm park in a field nearby. We find ourselves getting out of the truck and walking by moonlight over crunchy, brittle, winter-dried grass. Cash stays at my side, slowing his pace so that my short legs can keep up with his long ones. Still, the walk is arduous, even without the grass as high as it might be in the summer. Finally, we reach the road and people are lined up on either side with Holloway in the middle of it, right on the line that indicates no passing.

He waits a few more moments for people to make it from their cars to the spot we're at. I wonder how many of them are there because they think he might be onto something and how many people are there because they want to marvel at the freak show.

Either way, the crowd is vast. It seems like at least two-thirds of the people that attended the dinner tonight are here. Holly is a no show, though. But I spot Linda Stone and her daughter across the road. And I wonder if Karen Dunham is here.

Surely she is.

The four of us wait in silence. Cash stands beside me and I pull his jacket tighter around me. Sitting in the amphitheater was one thing, but being out here in the frigid night with nothing to shield me from the elements is something else. Even his winter-ready coat is taking a beating from the blasts of icy air.

Finally, satisfied with the crowd he draws, Harrison Holloway speaks. He reminds me of a circus ringleader and a conman rolled into one. Like one of those big cat people running a sanctuary/cult. I'm sure he wouldn't take kindly to my analysis. But I feel a swell of pride thinking that my dad might.

I'd give anything right now to know what my dad would make of this. Likely, he'd interpret it all as bullshit. A way for Holloway to get a place for himself back inside the Bigfoot community. But to what end? Holloway has to think that this could be national news or something. Or that he could get some monetary gain from it. He's not trying to solve Michael Berkley's disappearance out of the goodness of his heart. That's for sure. And I don't need a medium to tell me that my dad would feel the same way.

Holloway speaks.

"It was right here at the beginning of December that Michael Berkley went missing," he says.

A silence falls over the crowd.

That much is true, and it's a dark reality. Darker here in a small town than it would be in the city. People go missing there all the time, and those that remain rarely have to fear each of their neighbors in the aftermath.

"And there was a witness that night," Holloway says.

He points into the crowd and gestures for a woman to join him. Karen Dunham, I'm sure. The drunk that Clayton talked about.

"Here she is, folks. Traumatized by what she saw that night." A sob interrupts the silence. It turns into a howling cry. All eyes find their way to Linda Stone and her daughter Haley. Haley is bawling. "I know, folks," Holloway says, bringing the attention back to himself. "Losing Michael was hard on the entire community."

Linda whisks Haley away and her sobs grow more distant. Holloway seizes the opportunity to turn up the dramatics, feeding off of the crying teenager.

"But I'm here to solve this mystery," he says. I can't help but roll my eyes. I glance at Cash, but his face doesn't betray any such emotion. He's a better performer than I am. Clayton on my other side laughs. He mutters something to Lisa, and I don't hear her response. Holloway seems none the wiser, either. He goes on, telling us how it happened.

"That night, Karen saw something. She saw something big. A Sasquatch, people. And she saw Michael

Berkley follow it." A tittering of conversation ripples through the crowd. At least Holloway has a grasp on how to use the shock factor. The way he goes on, I feel like at any moment he's going to tell us that he actually has the Bigfoot himself and if we walk around the corner we can see it for the cheap price of one dollar per peek into his sideshow tent. But he doesn't.

Karen stands next to him now, seeming proud of what she's stirred up.

"Karen saw it that night because she parked by those trees in the field that all of you parked in tonight," Holloway says.

"What was she doing there?" someone asks, their voice echoing off the pavement and the trees that surround us.

"I was out for a drive," Karen says, but her speech slurs, even now. I feel a pang of embarrassment for her. The feeling that Holloway is exploiting her is strong.

A murmur goes through the crowd, people taking in this fresh evidence and synthesizing it to whatever ideas they might already have about Michael Berkley's disappearance.

I observe the pair of them carefully, Holloway and Karen Dunham.

What could she have to gain out of this? The answer is always money. Follow the money in any enterprise and you'll find what you're looking for.

But Holloway likely doesn't have the money to promise her much. But he would if this turned into the kind of story where he ended up on the Today Show and got a book deal.

I tuck the thought away for further analysis later. I'll bounce it off of Cash, I'm sure, when we have time to openly discuss all of this again.

"But enough talk, folks," Harrison Holloway says. "Let's see the reenactment." He turns to face the entrance to the farm. A metal building stands and parked next to it is a truck that I assume to be a representation of Michael Berkley's vehicle. I watch as it all plays out.

A guy, playing Michael Berkley, gets out of his truck and seems to see something down the road. Just then, a man in what can only be described as a King Kong costume grunts and knocks a piece of wood against a tree.

Michael runs after the creature and the creature lures him into the woods. Then the actor playing Michael lets out a bloodcurdling scream.

The whole thing would be laughable if there wasn't an actual missing person involved.

"Did he really just do that?" I mutter under my breath.

"Never put anything past Harrison Holloway," Cash mutters back.

"Now," Holloway says, taking the center of the road again, his stage for the moment. "I'll be presenting some ideas about where this Sasquatch might be tomorrow. And tomorrow night, we'll go looking for it."

The crowd breaks into applause and I can't believe what I'm hearing and seeing. They're all for it. Whether it's because they believe it has any merit or because they just think it's a great way to spend a Friday night, I'm not sure. Either way, the showman Holloway has got them in the palm of his hand.

My blood boils on behalf of my father. Holloway dismisses everyone, and people stand in groups talking. Some of them head for their cars. Clayton leads the way to the truck, obviously done with the whole thing, and probably relieved that they did no damage to his property. I walk beside Cash, both of us silent on the way back to the truck. We all get in and make the journey back to the house.

When we get out, Cash comes around to my side of the truck and grabs my arm.

"I'm gonna have a smoke," he tells Clayton.

"Knock yourself out, man," Clayton says, disinterested.

"You want one?" he asks me. I stare at him, confused for a moment, but then I realize he's trying to buy us a moment alone to talk.

"Yes," I say.

Clayton and Lisa disappear into the house and Cash leads me around back to the patio. There's a small, shielded area with a fire pit. It's gas and Cash turns it on. He finds a bluetooth speaker and turns that on, too, pairing it with his phone. He puts on some music.

"Background noise," he says, jerking his head at the house, indicating that it should help whatever we talk about out here remain private. I nod. Cash warms his hands by the fire and seems to collect his thoughts. I do the same, but I can't help myself from speaking first. All the emotions from the evening get the better of me. Thinking about how my father would feel. Thinking about how Karen Dunham is being exploited. Haley Stone's outburst and how much pain this has obviously caused the community. And Holloway at the helm of it all now. I really only have one thing to ask Cash, and I spit it out before he can say anything.

"What the hell was that?"

CHAPTER EIGHTEEN

"I'M NOT EVEN SURE, and I've seen Holloway at his worst," Cash says, holding his palms over the fire, absorbing the heat.

Back here, tucked away from the elements, though still outside, the cold isn't too bad.

I run my own hands over the fire, feeling it bite at my skin the same way the cold did back at the amphitheater. The long nights of winter always make me ache for the summer. And being out here, practically in the middle of nowhere, with Jack Frost as our only company, makes me miss it even more.

I tell myself every year I'll appreciate it, and every year I find myself bitching about the heat. Not this year. Not after seeing how cold it can really be in the great outdoors. Though, I have a feeling I've only just gotten a taste of that.

"What was he like when my dad dealt with him?" I ask Cash.

"Not so different from what you saw out on that road tonight," he says with disdain. He's got contempt for the guy and I don't blame him. Even being an outsider, I empathize with why people hate him.

"Why were so many people wanting to see what he had to say about Michael Berkley?" I ask. "Don't most of the people think he's full of it?"

"That doesn't stop him from putting on a good show, now does it?" Cash asks.

"You have a point there," I tell him.

That much is definitely true. If nothing else, tonight we did get a show.

Cash grows quiet for a moment and it occurs to me that the reason we came back here wasn't just to talk about Harrison Holloway's little performance tonight, though that's part of it.

"So, when are you going to ask Clayton about that stuff?" I probe. I know the topic is uncomfortable for Cash. Hell, it's uncomfortable for me. And I'm not even that good of friends with the guy. There's still something infinitely disconcerting about realizing that you might be spending your weekend in the home of a murderer though. That prompts me to ask something that I'd been biting my tongue about. "Do you think he's capable?"

I look up at Cash, over the fire. He stares at the flame, his face twisted in concentration, like maybe he can look at it from a certain direction and not feel like the answer to my question is *yes*. His pause is all I need. I don't need to know more. Or to know why. I nod my head silently.

"Well, that's heavy," I say, in an attempt to lighten the mood. Cash smiles slightly as he stares at the flame. Then he looks up at me.

"Have you ever known someone and known they were capable of something like that?" he asks. The question is startlingly intimate. Probably one of the most naked questions Cash has ever asked me. And instantly I know the answer. Probably one he's not expecting from me.

"I have, actually," I say. He raises an eyebrow.

"Hard to believe that Blair Graves, straight arrow, and all around good girl, could know someone like that," he remarks. There's curiosity in his statement.

"Noelle," I say.

"Your best friend?" he asks, his eyebrow arching higher.

"Not her," I go on. "Her cousin, Jenna."

I think about one of the reasons that Noelle and I are such good friends and it has to do with this very thing. Noelle knew darkness before I did and it bound us together. We understood one another in a way that other people didn't understand us.

"Did Jenna kill someone?" Cash asks.

"No," I say. "But she tried." He looks at me like I'm stripping right there in front of him. His face is shocked. "I guess I'm not such a straight arrow to have known her," I say with a smirk. "She gets out of prison this summer. Noelle's dreading it," I add.

"Why's she dreading it?" Cash asks.

"Noelle's testimony helped put her away and Jenna has a long memory and an ability to hold grudges that you wouldn't believe. I don't blame her for dreading it."

"You really are something," Cash remarks. And the way that the words come out, it makes me think he meant to keep them to himself.

"Why do you say that?" I ask.

"It's like just when you think you've peeled back the last layer, there's something else." He stares at me in the darkness. I feel a flush fan over my chest and cheeks.

"I could say the same about you," I tell him.

"Oh, there's nothing to me," he waves away the sentiment. "I'm simple."

"Hardly," I tell him. I think about going with him in the middle of the night to see his dad. To make sure he was okay. The way it pains him to think that Clayton could have done something to Michael Berkley. Cash doesn't have that many people left. He holds the ones he does have very close. And there's something about the way he smiles at me just then that makes me wonder if he counts me among their number.

"You know," he says, looking away from me, back

into the fire burning in front of him. "I'm really glad you left me that nasty comment." He smirks and looks up. I find a smile breaking across my face, because honestly, I am, too.

"Maybe it was fate," I tell him.

"Maybe so," he says. The pair of us sit there for a moment, looking at each other like that. An easy silence descends and I don't want the conversation to return to Michael Berkley or his lost lanyard and planner. I don't want to talk about how Clayton might be capable of murder. I want to talk about something else entirely and it almost bubbles up out of my chest when, from inside the house, we both hear yelling.

We lock eyes and both sit up straighter.

I make out Lisa's voice, loud and full of anger, not like I've heard her ever before.

"You never should have gotten involved with him," she shouts. Something breaks against the wall and Cash and I both jump. My eyes widen and I strain my ears to make out the rest of the fight.

"I did it for you!" Clayton shouts. Something else shatters.

"Should we do something?" I ask Cash. There's a look of concern on his face. "Let's go back inside. Be loud about it. Maybe they'll stop," I say.

"Good idea," he replies. And the pair of us head back to the front of the house and Cash makes a big performance of opening the glass storm door. He opens the wooden door behind it and clears his throat.

"That Holloway is a crazy son of a bitch, huh?" he says loudly in my direction.

"Totally nuts," I say equally as loudly.

Just then Lisa comes around the corner from the hallway that leads to the master bedroom. Her eyes are puffy with tears but she wears a smile, doing her best to hide it.

"I hope you guys had a good time today," she offers meekly. Clayton comes rushing out from the same hallway and grabs Lisa by the arm. Then he loosens his grip when he sees us. His eyes are wild, desperate. He runs a hand through his hair.

"Hell of a show tonight, huh?" he asks with a forced laugh. I nod.

"Hell of a show," Cash says pointedly. the four of us stand there for what seems like an eternity. I clear my throat. "I think we're going to head to bed," Cash says, cueing off of me. I nod and offer a smile to Clayton and Lisa, praying it doesn't seem disingenuous.

Praying that it doesn't seem like the smile of a woman who just listened to them argue from their back patio.

I take the stairs first, and hear Cash behind me. I reach for my doorknob and he grabs me, spinning me to face him.

"I'm going to try and find out what that was about," he tells me.

"Do you think you can?" I ask. He nods.

"Get some rest," he tells me. His hand is still on my arm and he gives it a squeeze. Then he drops it and turns to go back downstairs.

I watch as he reaches the landing and grabs the railing, disappearing down the stairs back into the common area of the house. I hope he's right and he can get some sort of information about why they were fighting.

The words Lisa said echo in my ears. Michael. They were fighting about Michael. And we need to find out why.

CHAPTER NINETEEN

I SLIP INTO MY BEDROOM, closing the door quietly behind me. I hear Cash padding downstairs and I press my ear to the wall nearest the stairs, trying to overhear anything I might. But all I'm able to make out are muffled words, two male voices.

So, at least Cash could talk to Clayton.

I realize I'm biting a hangnail as I stand there wondering if he might bring up the lanyard and planner with Clayton.

How might he react? What would I do if he confronted me with something like that? How would I react if I had some sort of guilt in the matter?

The thought occurs to me that things could turn nasty.

Surely they won't.

Maybe Cash won't even bring that stuff up tonight. He indicated he was more interested in finding out why Clayton and Lisa were fighting. And I feel like he could tell just by asking about that whether it had something to do with Michael's disappearance or not.

I sigh and resign myself to waiting. So, I pull my laptop out and sit it on the bed. I wash my face and slip into some flannel pajamas. The cold is pressing in at the windows tonight. I crawl onto the bed and pull the covers up around me, and then I put my laptop on my legs and open it up.

I search for Michael Berkley, just to see if they have published any new news articles in the last week or so. But the only recent one I find is the one I saw when we were on our way down here. I turn to social media and start looking for his accounts.

First, I find his Instagram, and it's full of photos of his students that are on the cross-country team. One post features Haley Stone crossing the finish line at a race. Another features the whole girls' team at a pizza restaurant, celebrating after that very race, I imagine.

There are posts with the boys' team, too. And then I dig into the comments.

There's one from Haley after Michael Berkley's disappearance. It's just a broken heart with the message hope you're okay.

Other comments are similar. Boys and girls from the cross-country teams wishing Mr. Berkley well, wherever he might be. I look over the rest of his Instagram and he seems like your everyday average high school teacher. There's nothing about the weed farm on his account, and I can imagine why there isn't. I remember hearing that the parents weren't keen on the idea that some teachers were making ends meet by working at what amounted to a recreational drug farm.

Oklahoma is still only medically legal, but they wrote the laws in a way where it might as well have been recreational. And getting a card is easy.

I know next to nothing about Michael Berkley, but he seems like an all-American guy. There are photos of him hiking. And then I spot one in the feed that stops me in my tracks.

It's taken at the spot where Cash and I found his belongings.

He's looking out over the valley, a hand shielding his eyes. The photo had to have been taken by another person or shot by Michael with a tripod. Could Clayton have been the one to take the photo? How good of friends were they? If they were, there was a good chance they went hiking elsewhere together. Remote locations.

I think about being up there with Cash. Even though it was close to the campground, the place was isolated. A delightful spot if you wanted secrecy. I switch over to Facebook after grabbing a screenshot of the Instagram picture that will sync with my phone. I'll show Cash in a little while. If he ever comes back up here tonight. I guess they're deep in conversation.

On Facebook, there's not much to see. Instagram was definitely where Michael Berkley hung out. I see that he's friends with Clayton and I find the weed farm listed as a place of employment for Michael. That hasn't changed. There is one thing, though, that catches my eye.

He changed his cover photo only a few days before his disappearance. It's white text on a black background. One of those non-poems that's just a sentence with no punctuation.

> TIMING IS EVERYTHING, AND
> SOMETIMES IT'S NOT ON YOUR SIDE

I stare at the quote, wondering why he posted it. It certainly seems ominous that he would post something like that only days before he would go missing.

Timing on what?

I think again about what we overheard when we were outside. Lisa saying that Clayton never should have gotten involved with him. She had to be talking about Michael. The tension in the car. The tension at the performance by Holloway. All of it had to do with Michael.

But something about my suspicions feels off. Like there's an enormous piece of the puzzle that I'm missing.

Why would Clayton have the motivation to make Michael disappear? Were they involved in some kind of shady venture together? And then Clayton saying he had done it for Lisa. But even if they were involved in something together, why would Clayton want to make Michael disappear?

I feel like after looking at all of this, I have more questions than answers.

My head spins with all of it, and all I really want to do is go to sleep. I close my laptop and place it back on the nightstand. I grab my phone and snuggle deeper under the covers. I go to my photos and stare at that picture of Michael standing on the ridge.

It had to have been taken in the summer. The grass was green, and he'd been wearing a short-sleeved t-shirt and hiking pants. No jacket. I'm about to tell myself that I have to let it go, at least for tonight, when I hear a tiny, careful knock on my door.

"Come in," I breathe.

Cash slips into my bedroom and runs a hand through his hair. He's still dressed in his jeans and thick coat, which he sheds quickly. He tosses it onto the end of my bed and I sit up.

"Well?" I ask him.

"Well," he starts, and then he sighs. "I don't know much more than we did when we were out back on the patio." He looks up at me, frustration plain on his features. I sigh then, too, equally frustrated. "However," he says. "I did get a bit out of him," Cash says and flashes me a winning smile. "I know why they were fighting at least," he says.

"And?" I prompt him, sitting up straighter.

For a moment, I feel like maybe we're just being

nosy. Just being busybodies. But then I think about what we found. Things that might be considered evidence in a missing person's case. The stress of all of it is going to catch up with me, I know. I just hope that happens when I'm far removed from this situation. Maybe back on my couch with a pint of ice cream and a glass of wine. I wait for Cash to speak.

"Lisa had a lot of trouble getting pregnant," Cash says. "Clayton grabbed us a couple of beers after she went on to bed and he told me about it. Said that things had been tight financially. That fertility treatments aren't cheap. Basically, he indicated they were in some financial trouble over it and that sometimes it got the best of them."

I furrow my brow.

"Jesus," I say. I feel a surge of sympathy for both of them.

"Took her a long time to get pregnant, I guess," Cash says, sympathy coloring his own tone. But then something comes back to me. What they were saying before we came inside.

"Didn't Lisa say something about how she wished Clayton had never gotten involved with him?" I ask.

"I remember that, too," Cash says. He rubs the five o'clock shadow on his face and I can hear the prickliness of it, the room is so quiet.

"Do you think he was talking about Michael?" I ask.

"He could have been," Cash says thoughtfully. But

I don't really know who else it could be. I make a non-committal sound, feeling like we're no closer to figuring this out than we were a few hours ago.

"You okay?" Cash asks me after I lose myself for a moment in thought. "I'm fine," I say, and offer a smile. He grabs his coat and walks over to the door.

"Get some sleep," he tells me and winks. Then he smiles at me, his gaze lingering a moment too long.

But before I can open my mouth to tell him the same, he's gone.

CHAPTER TWENTY

AFTER CASH LEAVES, I lie there, awake for some time. It's well into the wee hours of the morning before I drift off, but there's one thought that keeps circulating around my subconscious and it's the idea that somehow, Clayton has some involvement with Michael.

I think about what Cash told me, that Lisa and Clayton needed to pay for infertility treatments. And then something comes back to me.

When Clayton said there was really no telling what those guys got up to outside of work. That combined with the shady past Cash told me about makes me wonder if maybe Michael had played a role in getting Clayton the money for the treatments.

Finally, I do fall asleep, but when I wake, the only thing I want to do is talk to Cash about this revelation. It's not even dawn yet when my eyes shoot open, almost like my body slept reluctantly. I probably only got a couple of hours.

I throw back the covers and creep to my door, I open it as quietly as I can, and fortunately, the hinges don't creak. I slip over to Cash's door and I knock gently. Once, twice, three times. I hear him stirring, turning over in bed. For a moment, I wonder if I should wake him up. But my desire to tell him my thoughts about Clayton is too strong. I can't resist. I knock again and Cash groans behind the door. I push it in ever so slightly and lean my head around where I can see him.

"Hey," I whisper.

"Hmmph," he replies.

I slink into his room and shut the door behind me carefully, turning the knob slowly so the door doesn't click loudly as it closes.

"Are you awake?" I ask quietly, the words coming out in a hiss.

"Why?" Cash mumbles.

"I thought of something after you left my room last night," I tell him, my voice getting a little louder with impatience.

"It sounds dirty when you say it like that," Cash says, his face halfway buried in his pillow. I roll my eyes.

"Do you want to talk about it or not?" I demand.

Finally, he pops an eye open and looks at me, clearly irritated that I interrupted what little sleep he was getting. I understand, I barely got any myself. But this seems important. I cross my arms over my chest.

"Fine," he mutters, sitting up in bed and I realize that he's not wearing a shirt. My eyes widen, taking him in and feeling embarrassed at the blush on my cheeks. I swallow, my mouth suddenly dry. His chest is chiseled, the muscles rippling as he brings his hands to his face to rub the sleep away from his features. I clear my throat, an errant thought wondering what it might be like to run my hand over his torso. I quickly swallow it down, telling myself that such thoughts are ridiculous. Cash is my friend. And that's all we are.

Right?

His eyes meet mine, seemingly oblivious to the effect his half naked body is having on me. I shake my head and try to form a coherent sentence.

"I think we might be onto something with Clayton and Michael," I tell him. Instantly he perks up, like a dog hearing a dinner bell.

"What?" he asks.

"What if weed isn't the only thing Clayton is involved in?" I pose the question, hoping that Cash will come to the only logical conclusion possible. But it's also possible that he'll get defensive. This is one of his best friends.

Cash seems to roll this over, processing it now in the wee hours of the morning before dawn. He probably wishes I could have waited a little later to bring this to his attention. But his response comes as a relief.

"Great minds think alike," he tells me, his voice full of sleep. "I was thinking the same thing."

"And maybe that's how Clayton was able to pay for Lisa's fertility treatments?" I probe a little further.

"That was my thought, too," Cash says. "Those don't come cheap. And the big money will always be in the black market," he adds.

I feel relief, but at the same time, a sinking feeling in my stomach like a stone settling at the bottom of a cold pond. What are we going to do about it? What *can* we do about it? The idea that Clayton and Cash's friendship might not survive this occurs to me. It has to occur to Cash, too, just judging from the look on his face. He knows that if we dig too deep we may find something he never wanted to see.

"You can't just ignore it," I tell him. "Can you?"

"That's what I'm trying to decide," he tells me. And once again, like last night, his jaw clenches, the muscles dancing under his skin as he works the question over in his mind. I don't know what to say. In my gut, I know the moral thing to do is to chase this down. And I don't know if I can let it go. Someone is missing and we have evidence that might lead the police in a different direction. A direction that might help them find Michael Berkley.

But is it the right thing to do? My gut tells me it is. But that's easy for me to say. I'm so far removed from this emotionally that it's easy to have clarity. Cash isn't. I leave him to his thoughts, and say a rare and silent prayer that he'll see reason. I am the straight arrow after all.

I don't sleep in. Instead, I go back to my room and stay wide awake, combing back over the articles I found about Michael Berkley at the beginning of all of this. I go back to his Instagram profile, trying to find some sort of clue that will tell me who took that picture of him on the ridge that Clayton and Cash used to frequent. There's a light pink sliver in the corner of the photograph but nothing significant. I lock my phone as dawn breaks. I lay there, watching the room slowly start to light up with the sun coming up outside. And then I get dressed, knowing I can't just sit here.

Maybe there's some way to figure out who took that picture.

Around seven I head downstairs and grab a glass of orange juice. I stand at the counter, sipping it, lost in deep thought over all of this. I'm standing there, sipping my drink, when Clayton comes walking out of the hallway and spots me.

"Good morning," he says.

"Good morning," I say back, suddenly feeling like I better keep my mouth shut. Like if I don't, I might accidentally say something that will give away the fact that I'm concerned he might have had something to do with Michael Berkley's disappearance.

Clayton gets the coffee maker started and heads over to the counter opposite the one I'm standing against. My eyes flit around the room, trying to find something to land on and wishing he wouldn't make any attempt at small talk. But somehow, the silence is worse. And I break it. Against my better judgment.

"Quite a sight last night, huh?" I ask, coming at it obliquely. Maybe if I can get him to talk about Harrison Holloway he'll slip up and say something.

"Holloway?" he asks, clarifying. I nod.

"He's such a joke," Clayton says as the coffee brews and the smell of the grounds starts to fill the kitchen. "More of a hassle than anything," he adds. "The only reason I went down there was because of what Lisa said. I didn't want him poking around at the farm stirring shit up."

I take another sip of my orange juice, wondering what things were like when the sheriff's department was investigating his operation. But before we can get into any conversation of real substance, I hear Cash's heavy footsteps jogging down the staircase, obviously with a pep in his step that he wasn't feeling when I went to visit him this morning. When he comes around the corner into the kitchen, he's wearing a sweater and jeans. And he's barefoot.

"Smelled the coffee," he says by way of greeting. Clayton gets the pot and pours them both a cup. "Heard you guys talking about Holloway," Cash says to Clayton but gives me a pointed look that makes me think he doesn't appreciate me trying to do any of my own investigating.

Clayton reiterates what he was saying to me. Cash

agrees, saying the whole thing was a performance. That he just wants the spotlight again. They start speculating that Karen Dunham didn't even see anything at all.

She might not have, I think. But it doesn't change the fact that at the beginning of December, Michael Berkley went missing, Bigfoot involved or not.

After breakfast, Clayton breaks the news to us that they aren't going to go to the festival with us.

"Everything alright?" Cash asks, sounding concerned. I wonder if it's about the fight they had last night. But Clayton gives another explanation out of earshot of Lisa.

"I think yesterday really wore her out," Clayton offers for an explanation.

I imagine the fighting wore her out for sure, I think. But he gives no indication that the fighting had anything to do with why Lisa might not be in a jovial mood today. And I haven't seen her since we got up.

I think about the sound of breaking glass last night and wonder just how bad the fight might have gotten. I wonder if they fight a lot. That was one thing I was lucky about with my father. He never raised his voice or laid a hand on either of us. He would just be silent, which, in the years after his alleged passing, seemed like it might have been the worst thing he could have done. Somehow the silence seemed worse than harsh words or a vase hitting the wall. The silence made me feel like he didn't care.

Not that flying glass would have done much to make me feel loved, either. Maybe we always think that however we had it was worse than everybody else. I remember thinking my friends with divorced parents were lucky, since they still had their two biological parents plus their step-parents. But I would have hated that growing up, just like all my friends with divorced parents did. Maybe we're just always wishing for what we don't have. But before I can get too far down the rabbithole of my childhood Cash interrupts my thoughts.

"You about ready to head over there?" he asks me. I snap back to reality and nod my head.

"Yeah, I'm ready," I tell him. And then I offer Clayton a small smile before scurrying out of the kitchen and away from his piercing gaze.

I'm kind of glad for us to be without him for the day. His presence is intense. And it feels even more so now that Cash and I think we're onto something. The whole vibe has been off since last night. Since he and Lisa were fighting.

Cash grabs a messenger bag of his that sits at the bottom of the staircase. I grab a heavier jacket that I brought and together we head out the door toward his pickup truck. As soon as both doors shut I look at him, slipping my sunglasses on.

"Is it just me or was that tense?" I ask.

"It wasn't just you," he says, staring back at the house from behind a pair of Raybans. "Something is up with him."

Cash starts the truck and throws it into reverse and we head for the gravel drive that leads back out to the road.

Together, Cash and I drive back over to the church. The crowd seems just as strong this morning, as though everyone who turned out last night came back to get a full picture of exactly what Harrison Holloway intended to paint for them. I grab my phone and pull up the schedule as Cash parks us in the back of the campground lot.

Even though we're early, a lot of people are earlier. I look at the schedule again in an attempt to see if Charlie has finally come clean to the masses that Harrison Holloway is here. But alas, there's still no new information.

As Cash kills the engine I say to him, "I guess they just aren't going to put Holloway on the website."

"Maybe Charlie thinks that makes it more acceptable somehow," Cash muses. "Maybe he thinks that if he doesn't put him on the schedule, he can't really be held responsible for it in some daring feat of stretching his logical abilities." He looks over at me. "But I bet when we walk in that building, Holloway's name will be on the schedule up front."

I don't have to take Cash's word for it, because when we walk back into the church, he's right. Front and center for today's lineup is Holloway, right before lunch.

"I suppose he's going to present more of his findings from last night," I say, somewhat to myself, but Cash catches it.

"Oh, I'm sure we'll get to hear about all of his whackadoodle theories about how Michael Berkley went missing, Blair." I turn to Cash, my brow furrowed. I'm a little surprised.

"You don't think there's a chance that he disappeared because of Bigfoot?" I ask. Cash is a logical person, but he wants to believe. And I can't imagine how, in this situation, where his friend might have some culpability in it all, that he wouldn't want to make this his front and center stance on things.

"Sometimes when it walks like a duck, and talks like a duck, it ain't a chicken, Blair," he says. I look at the schedule, seeing who's up first and it's a lady Bigfooter. My attention perks up at that.

The field seems dominated by male researchers. There are plenty of women here, but I wonder how many of them hold respected positions within the community. Immediately, I want to see her speak.

"I want to go to that one," I tell Cash. I point at her name. Katie Reinhart.

"Katie's a good researcher," Cash says. "She's even a university professor in California. Anthropology. She's more respected here at this conference than she is in her own department. Thankfully, she has tenure."

I raise an eyebrow. I hadn't thought about that. But being an expert in a field like this is probably like telling your anthropology colleagues that you were abducted by aliens last night. I don't imagine that the wider zoological and anthropological communities are very open to the things that the people here might present to them. It makes me want to talk to Katie Reinhart one on one, even though I haven't heard a word she has to say yet.

"Do you want to go with me?" I ask Cash.

"I wouldn't miss it," he says with a smile.

I hate what his smile does to me. And I hate that I'm thinking things about Cash that are only going to lead to a world of hurt. I feel a twisting in my gut at the thought. I remind myself again that we're just friends and that's how things are going to stay if I know what's good for me.

I lead the way and we head back to the room where Katie is presenting. Cash and I snag two seats in the back, nestled almost on top of each other in the packed room.

A blonde woman at the front of the room is gathering some things together, papers and what not that I assume are going to be part of her presentation. I glance around at the fellows in the audience. Men and women are gathered, ready to hear what Katie has to say. I lean over to Cash.

"Is she a fan of Holloway's?" I whisper, hoping that no one overheard me. The last thing I want to do is get into an argument with a stranger over the guy, only for the stranger to realize who I am. So far, I've been rather lucky in that only a couple of people recognized me and they've been incredibly nice. Even if they do like Holloway and what he has to say here, they seem to have respect for my dad. Thank God for little favors.

"Quite the opposite, actually," Cash says. "She's well-respected in the field. Leads some expeditions in northern California from time to time. She's even been down here in Oklahoma investigating Area X."

"What's that?" I ask. But before Cash can give me an overview of the topic, Katie clears her throat into the microphone. The room goes silent, probably as eager, if not more so, as I am to hear what she's got to say.

I have to admit that from the time Cash invited me down here to now, my mind is opening up a little bit. People take this creature very seriously. I think about Linda Stone's nephew giving his testimony as to what he experienced. It was clear that during that whole experience, he feared for his life.

"It's good to be back in Oklahoma," Katie says. Everyone gives a round of applause, proud of our home state. Cash and I even join in. As the crowd quiets down, she goes on. "As most of you know, I'm Katie

Reinhart and I'm an anthropologist at the University of Northern California. And I make a habit of studying Bigfoot."

I sink into my seat and get absorbed in Katie's presentation. And for a moment I think that there might be something magical about all of this after all.

CHAPTER TWENTY-ONE

BY THE TIME Katie gets done with her presentation, I'm hooked.

She's legit.

She presented all kinds of biological evidence about why the footprint castings that people show are mostly real. She has analyzed a ton of them, basing her theory off of how known primates walk and where their weight distributes in their prints. She's pretty much got me convinced that Bigfoot isn't just a figment of everyone's wild imagination. She's got me thinking that it's out there. That whatever Linda Stone's nephew saw was absolutely real.

"What'd you think?" Cash asks me as I sit there, staring up at Katie in something akin to awe.

"That was really fucking cool," I tell him. A smile breaks over his face. Like this might have been what he was hoping for all along when he first asked me to come down here with him. It makes the grin on my own face widen until my cheeks hurt with the force of it.

"Thank you," I say. "For asking me to come down here with you."

"Of course," he says, that same easy smile on his face that gets me every time. "I wanted you to get to experience it."

Just then someone interrupts us, recognizing Cash from his YouTube channel and ghost and monster hunting adventures. And I take the opportunity to excuse myself and go make conversation with Katie. She fascinates me.

She's a small woman, maybe in her late thirties with ash blonde hair that falls around her face in a short bob. It's a haircut that's both cut and utilitarian, probably easy to take care of when she's out on an expedition, like in Area X. Which she explained to be a portion of Oklahoma that is so remote, it's highly active with Bigfoot sightings. And it's private, so researchers can go out there and stay for months at a time.

She's smiling, talking to another festival goer and I wait my turn, feeling a little star struck even though I've only just found out who she was and what she's about.

"Thank you," she says with a wide grin to the person she's been talking to and they move on. She begins to gather up her papers on the table in front of herself.

"Hi," I say, and she looks up.

"Hello," she says cheerily.

"I just wanted to tell you how much I enjoyed your presentation," I tell her.

"Well, thank you!" she says, as if it's the first time she's hearing it. She's incredibly gracious. Totally opposite vibes from Harrison Holloway last night. I really like her already.

"I'm just—"

"Wait a second," she says, measuring my features. "You're Graham Graves's daughter, aren't you?"

I blush deeply.

"You caught me," I say with an uneasy smile.

I'm not sure what her relationship might have been to him. But I would assume dad would have taken her research seriously if she's always been this meticulous. To my relief, a huge smile breaks across her face.

"Your dad was a great man," she says. "I recognize you from the magazine spread he did with you kids."

I was only eighteen when that happened. It was just a bit of time after that when he disappeared. But the years all seem to run together in my mind. Like a glob of goo, folding in on itself. Somehow, when tragedy strikes over and over again, it changes time for you. It slows it down and speeds it up all at once and makes some moments indistinguishable from others.

I smile, trying to be gracious myself.

"You know," Katie says. "I'm doing an expedition tonight if you'd like to come."

My eyes widen at the possibility. I'm hardly prepared to go out into the woods and know virtually nothing that would help me keep myself safe out there, but I want to go, nonetheless. A break from the house with Clayton and Lisa would be nice. Just to get away from the tension for a few hours. Kind of like an extension of today, just Cash and I at the festival.

"I have a friend with me," I tell her. "Is it alright if I bring him?"

"Sure," she says and then starts gathering her notes again. "We'll meet out front of the church around seven tonight." I nod, feeling giddy like a high school girl that just made a new friend. I smile at Katie and then turn, heading back for Cash.

When I find him, his admirers are gone and he's waiting for me, watching from the back of the room, a smirk on his face.

"Guess what," I tell him. He arches an eyebrow.

"I don't know," he says. "What?"

"I just got us a spot on an expedition tonight with Katie Reinhart," I say excitedly. He looks at me like he doesn't recognize me for a moment.

"Are you the same Blair Graves that left me that nasty comment on YouTube?" he teases. "The same one that would have rather died a month ago than admit her house was infested with a very angry spirit?"

There's a playful gleam in his eye and I smile back at him.

"I suppose I am," I tell him. And then he looks at

me with something close to pride. And it feels good. Really good.

He gets up and I lead the way back to the atrium, neither of us saying much. I want to hold onto this moment. This feeling that I could be someone other than myself. Other than the girl who resented everything that her father held dear. Maybe I could be someone that embraced the things he did. And maybe if I did, just for a little bit, I'd feel closer to him. Maybe I'd be able to understand why he did things the way he did. Maybe not. But it's worth a shot.

Cash and I attend another talk before it's time for Holloway to speak. this one is good, but not nearly as compelling as Katie Reinhart's presentation. Maybe I'm biased since I'm apparently a fan girl of hers now, but I doubt it.

The evidence Katie presented was so neutral. So scientific. There wasn't wild speculation. Just theories based on things we already know about primates and the natural world around us.

I brace myself for whatever Holloway is going to have to say. I can't imagine that any of it is going to be worth noting down. All of it is likely going to be one conspiracy theory after another about how and why Michael Berkley disappeared.

I wonder for a moment what my dad would have made of it. All of it. The festival, the presenters, the disappearance of Michael Berkley, Clayton's shady past. What dots might he have connected?

I wish I could ask him.

It's a recurring thought that I seem to keep having. Wanting to connect with him. Feeling like I missed that boat. I should have tried harder when he was alive. I've blamed him for a long time, but how much of the fault is at my feet?

The second presentation ends and Cash looks over at me.

"Are you okay?" he asks. I glance at him and swipe a tear forming in the corner of my right eye.

"Fine," I try to assure him with a smile.

"Are you about to cry?" he asks. But there's something gentle about the question. It doesn't come out as teasing or accusatory. There's genuine concern in his voice.

"No," I say, but my voice breaks. And then the tears start coming for real.

"Here, come with me," Cash says, helping me up and out of the room. He leads me back to the atrium and then outside on the back side of the church. No one is out here with us. Everyone is shuffling into the next presentation they want to see, which I'm assuming for most of the people here is Holloway's.

I lean against the cold brick and I can feel it through my jacket. I wipe the tears from both of my eyes now.

"Are you sure you're okay?" Cash asks again. "I won't tell anyone if you're not," he says, teasing me gently.

"I just got a little overwhelmed in there," I say.

"Everything okay?" he asks. He places a hand on my shoulder and stoops to look into my eye, almost as if I'm a child. It makes me smile.

"I was just thinking about my dad. What he'd make of everything going on this weekend." I sniffle, regaining my composure.

"I think about that a lot, too," Cash says softly, standing back up. "Your dad was a great man, Blair," he says. "I took a lot of advice from him. And I wouldn't be where I'm at today, doing what I'm doing if it weren't for him."

"What do you think he would think of all of this?" I ask.

"Well, for starters," he says with a smirk. "I think he'd be elated that his daughter scored a spot on Katie Reinhart's Bigfoot team." He punches me lightly in the arm. "Come on," he says. "We're going to miss the show."

CHAPTER TWENTY-TWO

WE HEAD into the main hall of the church, where Holloway is going to be giving his presentation. The pews are packed and murmuring ripples through the crowd before he comes in. Cash and I find a spot in one of the back pews. Every other possible seat is already taken.

Without actual chairs under our asses, my leg is pressed against Cash's, even more closely than it was at the amphitheater. I'm suddenly conscious of the warmth that radiates off of him. I absorb it, wishing that I could reach for his hand. I want more of the comfort he offered me outside. I want him to tell me that everything is going to be alright and that we're going to figure this out. Figure out the right thing to do.

But I resist the urge to reach for him. I resist the urge to ask for reassurance. Instead, I stare at the pulpit, waiting for Holloway to take his place.

Cash shifts in his seat, and as if he read my mind, he stretches out his left arm and puts it around me casually, resting it on the back of the pew. I stiffen, then tell myself it's because he's huge. He's cramped in seating like this. There's nothing more to it and I'd be a fool to read into it. Besides, we need to be focusing on whatever that buffoon gets up there to say. And it's not long before the object of our attention walks up to the pulpit.

Holloway is dressed much the same as he was the opening night of the festivities. Plaid shirt and jeans. His gray hair swept over on one side. His piercing blue eyes peer out into the crowd. I watch him as he begins.

"Well, I was going to make a presentation about the research I've been doing in the past few years," he says. "But there's a more pressing matter that needs my attention, and it needs yours as well." Everyone is still. A murmur goes through a pew a few rows in front of us. I try to make out what they're saying but I can't. Then Holloway begins to speak again. "Michael Berkley, beloved high school teacher, went missing only a month and a half ago," he points to the screen behind him that suddenly is illuminated with the projected image of Michael Berkley. It's identical to the picture on the lanyard that we found.

I swallow, my mouth going dry.

"This was his faculty picture for this current school year," Holloway says. the crowd watches his perfor- mance with rapt attention. Cash and I are no exception. "Now, as many of you know, Michael went missing from the weed farm outside of town. His pickup truck was found there, but he and his belongings were not."

Another slide pops onto the screen, showcasing the picture of Michael Berkley's truck that was featured in a news article. The picture was taken the next day, with midday sunshine making the truck clear for all to see. It's the only one in the lot in the picture.

"Some of you may be aware that Michael was the cross country coach," Holloway goes on. "And he was very well-liked by everyone in town. There was no reason for someone like Michael to go missing, except for one."

With a flair for the dramatic, Harrison Holloway points to the next slide that pops up on the screen. It's the muddy image of what I assume is supposed to be a footprint. But in the picture, Holloway's boot is next to it, and his foot is considerably smaller.

"This was a footprint discovered a few days later, not by the police, but by my team, after we were contacted by Karen Dunham to investigate what the police refused to look at."

I glance over at Cash, and he's still staring at Holloway, transfixed with his brows furrowed in concentration.

"The footprint is a little hard to make out, so let me help you folks." A yellow line pops up on the next slide, outlining the footprint for all to see. It looks to me like wishful thinking and I don't see any of the markings that were present in anything that Katie Reinhart presented. It looks like an impression in the mud that could have been made by anything or anyone. It's so distorted that it's hard to even tell what might have been there to leave a track like that. But Holloway seems hellbent on making his point, no matter how farfetched.

"Now, I want to have Karen come up here and tell you all what she saw that night. The report that was completely thrown out by the police and sheriff's department."

Holloway steps back and holds out the microphone to a woman that comes across the stage to him. She's slender and looks like she's had a rough life. And when she begins to speak, there's a slurring to her voice that makes me think she might have done permanent damage to her brain over the years with how much alcohol she's consumed.

It makes me sad. And angry.

I get this overwhelming sense that Holloway is exploiting her and she's so disliked in town that no one really cares. A flare of righteous anger burns in my chest cavity. But she takes the microphone and begins to speak despite my feelings.

"I know what I saw that night," she says, her enunciation not the most precise. "I saw a Sasquatch. And you all know that they're around here. I know every one of you has seen one or heard one. I saw one that night. And I saw it lead Michael Berkley into the woods."

I think about the things that we heard from everyone else, and from the news articles. Berkley's footprints weren't tracked into the woods. they abruptly ended at the entrance to the forest. Maybe swallowed by time and nature, but the dogs didn't track him any further.

"I know what I saw," Karen reiterates. And Holloway steps up to save her from herself, taking the microphone. She reluctantly gives it up to him.

"This is an honest woman," Holloway says. Someone snorts out a laugh from the audience. I feel for her instantly. I want to tell them to leave her the fuck alone and for Holloway to back off. If he wants to continue this merry charade, he needs to leave Karen Dunham out of it.

She sits down and I feel my uneasiness ebb away. At least now it's just Holloway up there, even though the whole thing has become a spectacle. He goes on.

"There's something out there, folks, and it got Michael Berkley," he says.

I chance a look over at Cash but he's still got that same, furrowed brow look going on, deep in concentration about whatever Holloway is going to say next. I turn back to face our speaker.

Holloway goes on to point out more pieces of "evidence" that Sasquatch had something to do with Michael Berkley's disappearance. All of it seems about as compelling as the indistinguishable footprint that was supposedly left behind by the creature. But people are still sitting, listening with all the attention they have to give. I guess I shouldn't judge them too harshly because I'm sitting here listening with all the attention I have to give, too.

Finally, Holloway starts to wrap things up, and I'm relieved. Ready to be done with this. But then he says something I wasn't expecting.

"Tonight," he says. "We're going to go out into the woods and look for this thing. So if you want justice for Michael or have a desire to go hunting for Bigfoot, join us," he concludes.

The crowd begins to break up, most of the people heading for the door. But a few walk up to the table to talk to Holloway or to register for his expedition, I'm not sure. Either way, the crowd gets more and more sparse. Finally, Cash and I stand up just as the few last people are leaving. As I turn to head for the door, I hear Holloway's voice.

"Blair?" he asks. "Is that you?"

His voice isn't warm. It's mean. It's full of venom and a promise for something worse. I turn to face him and Cash steps up, putting himself between us.

"I remember your daddy didn't like me too much," Holloway says.

"For good reason," Cash offers.

"I wasn't talking to you, son," he says.

"Well, I was talking to you," Cash counters.

"Pretty girl like you shouldn't be out here in the boonies," Harrison Holloway says to me. I swallow, my mouth feeling dry all over again.

"Leave her alone," Cash says, fighting this for me. I reach out an arm to stop him.

"You listen to me," I tell Holloway. His eyes widen as I speak. "You aren't going to intimidate me just like you didn't intimidate my dad. And whatever is behind this, we're going to figure it out and expose you as a fraud once and for all," I tell him, now the venom is dripping from my lips. Holloway narrows his eyes.

"Well see about that," he says.

"Let's go," I tell Cash, before he can start something.

CHAPTER TWENTY-THREE

"I CAN'T BELIEVE THAT GUY," Cash says, steaming with anger as I yank him out of the room and into the hallway that leads to the back door of the church. I think it's time to go outside again. This time not for my sake, but for his.

I've never seen him pissed like this. He looked like he wanted to rip Holloway's head right off his body, and with as huge as Cash is, he could do it. Easily. Five times over.

There's something about the idea that's kind of hot. No, that's bad. I shouldn't be thinking that. It would not be hot if Cash got arrested for assault. At all. In fact, it would complicate matters more than they already are.

"Hey," I say to him after I get him outside. He's clenching his jaw again, though this time his teeth seem to be working overtime, grinding against each other.

The tension there from the other night seems mild compared to this. It occurs to me that if Cash wanted to hurt someone, there's nothing I could do to stop him. The thought is kind of terrifying. Like being in the presence of a tiger or some other large beast capable of devastating violence.

But I can't imagine Cash doing that. Not unless someone's life was at stake. However, the anger in his eyes is making me doubt myself on that.

"I'm glad you said what you did say to him," Cash says. "Your dad would have liked that," he adds, the tension on his face slowly breaking, replaced by a grin. "Sorry I nearly lost it on the guy," he adds.

"It's okay," I tell him. "I just wanted to be sure you were okay."

"I'm fine. I probably don't need to see Holloway again today but I'm fine," he adds with a chuckle. I smile at him.

"Who knew that Bigfooting was so rife with dramatics," I tease Cash.

"All the best weird little subcultures are," he says with an easy smile. the easiest he's giving me so far since we've left the room where Holloway was presenting. I smile back at him.

"So what should we do to pass the rest of the day?" I ask.

"I think maybe we should do some looking around. Maybe ask some people some questions. I kind of want to get Karen Dunham alone," he says. I nod.

It's a solid plan, because we don't really know all that much about what went down that night.

"I think we need to get an official perspective, too," I tell Cash. That makes him smile.

"My very next suggestion," he confirms my idea. "And then maybe we can start to piece this thing together," he concludes. I nod, and we part ways, searching for Karen across the building.

Cash takes the north end and I take the south end. Even though he said he didn't want to run into Holloway, he also said that he thought it would be better for him to run into the guy than for me to run into him. And I can't help but agree. He gave me the creeps back there and I don't relish another moment alone with the guy.

I head for the front of the building, where people are milling about, some of them discussing plans for lunch and I catch other murmurs of people discussing plans to join Holloway on his expedition later. I wonder how many of them take him seriously. How many of them find him amusing. And how many of them think he's a stain on the Bigfoot community.

I walk around by the bathrooms and spot Karen, standing alone near the entrance to the women's room. She doesn't seem to be waiting to enter as several people go in front of her, half of them going on to the men's restroom and half of them going into the women's. I stop and take a drink from the fountain across from her and then I sidle up beside her and lean against the wall, doing my best to seem non-threatening, and hoping that she didn't see the exchange with Holloway that I just had. I don't think that would do much in the way of building her confidence in me or making her think I'm someone to be trusted. She glances over at me and I look at her. I seize the opportunity.

"Hi," I say. "My name is Blair." She eyes my hand suspiciously as I hold it out.

"You a reporter?" she asks.

"I'm not," I assure her.

That seems to set her somewhat at ease. She looks at me now with something more like curiosity than suspicion that I'm out to get her. I imagine there have been reporters that wanted her story just for the sensationalism of it.

"Then what are you doing here talking to me?" she asks with a crooked smile. There's warmth in her eyes that makes me think people aren't often kind to her and there's something about me that she thinks she can trust. It hurts. It's painful to think that's what her life is like. And it makes fury rise again inside me at the idea that Holloway is exploiting her.

"I heard you back there," I say. "I just wanted to see if I could talk to you about what you saw."

"So you can make fun of me?" she asks.

"No," I say, trying to project kindness into my voice. "I just want to hear the whole story of what you saw that night. I'm not a reporter and your story is safe with me."

Karen seems to think this over and finds it acceptable.

"Do you want to come with me so my friend can hear too?" I ask. "He's an expert," I fib. Cash might not be a Bigfoot expert, but he's got a hell of a lot more integrity than Harrison Holloway ever will. Finally, she nods, after thinking it over. And I take her hand, leading her back to where Cash and I agreed to meet up.

Karen and I stand there for a few minutes, waiting for Cash, but then he appears, coming out of the side doors of the church. I smile and wave at him but he's already got us in his sights. He holds out his hand to introduce himself to Karen.

"Nice to meet you," Cash says.

"Nice to meet you, too," Karen counters.

"We just wanted to ask you to tell us your story, just the way it happened that night," Cash says. "We're trying to get to the bottom of things."

"That's what Harrison says," Karen tells us. "But I don't think he's doing much."

"I'm sorry to hear that," I tell her. "Really, we would be so grateful to hear the entirety of events that night."

Karen nods, and then she launches into the story

again, repeating some parts from when she was on stage.

"I was there, parked late at night," she says. "Just wanted to get out of the house," she adds. "I was by some trees and I could see the entrance to the farm. Michael was parked there. I saw him get out. And I saw something big take him into the woods after he walked a few steps down the road. And I'm telling you, it was a Bigfoot," she concludes.

"Did the Bigfoot pick Michael up?" Cash asks.

"Yes," Karen says. "He grabbed him around the neck and started pulling him toward the forest. Then he picked him up, Michael was kicking."

"How long did you stay there," Cash asks.

"I was scared. Frozen in place, I guess," Karen says.

"So you stayed where you were parked for a little bit?" Cash asks.

"Yes," Karen agrees.

"What did you see after that?" I ask.

"I saw someone pick Bigfoot and Michael up in a truck," Karen says. "But Harrison says I probably just got spooked and made that part up." She looks unsure of herself.

"What?" I ask, not sure that I heard her right.

"Someone came and picked them up. Two people," she says. I look at Cash.

"Is there anything else you can tell us?" Cash asks Karen.

"I don't think so," she says, a sad look crossing her face. I wonder if she ever told the police this part.

We let Karen excuse herself and she heads back to the building. Cash looks at me, excitement in his eyes. "Well hell," he says. "I think we're onto something."

CHAPTER TWENTY-FOUR

I LOOK AT CASH, the excitement in his eyes is infectious. This is the first thing we've heard since finding the lanyard and the planner that points us in any direction. He pulls me closer and whispers.

"So she actually saw someone that night. Three someone's, apparently," he says.

"That's what I'm gathering," I tell him.

"Which kind of blows Holloway's Bigfoot story out of the water," he says. "Most Sasquatch aren't known for getting into a car with someone."

"One would think," I say, agreeing with him.

"Holloway's only going to want to pay attention to the portions that fit with what he wants to tell people. And seeing a Bigfoot drag a guy into a pickup truck isn't something that will help Holloway get his name out there front and center." Cash seems to be thinking it over.

"No one in town seems to have wanted Michael to disappear," I say. "He seems to have been well-liked by everyone," I add.

"You're right about that," Cash says. His brow is twisted in concentration and I'm sure mine is as well.

Who would have wanted Michael to disappear? The question points me in an unpleasant direction that I was hoping we could avoid.

"How can we find out if Clayton really had some shady dealings with Michael?" I blurt the question out, not waiting for Cash to confirm that his thoughts are going the same direction as mine. Cash thinks this over.

"We'll figure something out," he says. I nod. I trust him. Now more than ever, even though I was having my doubts earlier in the trip. It feels like we're in this together now, however deep that might be. "But for now, I think we need to get ready to go out tonight with Katie Reinhart," he says. "Maybe in the midst of all this chaos, you'll get to have a nice experience," he adds with a smile.

"I'm not sure how nice of an experience it's going to be being out in the woods late at night," I tell him. But I'd be lying to myself if I said that I wasn't excited.

Things are tense at the house when we get back and Cash and I decide to go up to his room and figure out what equipment of his we're going to take tonight. This is totally out of my comfort zone, even with the ghost hunting I did over the holidays. Bigfoot is some- thing else entirely, I'm discovering. And it's kind of amazing how vast and varied people's theories about him are.

But that was one of the things that I liked about Katie Reinhart. To her, Bigfoot is a flesh and blood creature that's just waiting to be discovered. She made a point in her presentation about the population required to support generations. And she said it was only a thousand or so.

Which makes it more realistic to me that Bigfoots could be out there in the wild, breeding, and roaming through densely forested terrain. It seems a lot more likely than if Bigfoot were say, an alien that visited people only in Las Vegas.

Cash pulls out a few different cameras and decides that this will make some good footage for his channel. I agree with him and he gets out the FLIR camera. I'm familiar with it from our usage of it in my house. It picks up heat signatures and looks like something that would be used by the miliitary. I'm sure it is.

Cash brings out a parabolic dish and hooks it up to his Zoom recorder, which is a fancy high dollar field recorder. The parabolic dish will let us pick up on anything that might be within a certain radius and still pretty far away.

"Do you think we need anything else?" I ask, already a little overwhelmed at the amount of equipment he wants to take into the field. It looks heavy, and I'm guessing that where we're going, there aren't going to be a lot of marked trails. Meaning that the terrain will be difficult enough to navigate without fancy equipment. But the thought doesn't seem to phase Cash, and he's done this before, so I trust him. It's still a little daunting, though. Thinking about being out in the woods. I guess I won't really know what it's like until I get out there. Just then, Clayton hollers from downstairs.

"Hey!" he shouts. Cash looks up at me then heads over to the door. He opens it and I hear the sound of Clayton coming up the stairs. He reaches the door and leans in. "I hear the two of you are going out into the woods tonight," he says.

His demeanor is less tense than earlier. Maybe he and Lisa are back on even ground. I hope they are.

"That's the rumor," Cash says with an easy smile.

"We're going into town to do some grocery shopping if you guys need anything," Clayton says.

Cash shakes his head, indicating he's good. But he looks at me as if to ask if I need anything.

"I'm fine," I tell Clayton and smile at him. He returns it, seemingly in a better mood than he's been in in the last forty-eight hours. He nods and shuts the door behind him, heading down the stairs, taking them two at a time from what I can hear.

"Well," Cash says. "Someone made up with his wife," he smirks.

"Do you think everything's okay?" I ask.

"It certainly seems like it," Cash says. I nod. That's good enough for me. And then something occurs to

Cash. I watch the sparkle in his eye that he gets when he has an idea. I arch an eyebrow in question.

"Wait," he says. Then he walks over to the door and opens it, listening. I hear the sound of a truck starting in the drive and heading out. Cash looks back at me. "Come on," he says. And I follow him out of the room and down the stairs.

Cash turns at the hallway, heading back toward Clayton and Lisa's bedroom. Then he makes a right turn and we head into Clayton's office. It's a large room with a beautiful oak desk in the center. Lots of dead animals line the shelves and the walls. A green banker's lamp sits on the desk, along with a slew of papers.

Cash goes around the desk and carefully starts looking through things. I follow his lead and start looking around the room, not really believing what I'm doing. Going through someone's private belongings, looking for signs that person is a killer. It seems absurd and at the same time, I'm afraid of what we might find.

Cash rifles through drawers and finally, he stops, grabbing something.

"Blair," he says. "Look."

I come over to his side. It's an envelope. And on the back it bears Clayton's name. The handwriting looks like it belongs to a man. It's all capitals and very boxy. Cash opens it and takes the letter inside out. And then he reads it aloud.

"Dear Clayton," he says. "Thank you so much for

your recent kindness. I will be forever in your debt. Michael Berkley."

"That's it?" I ask. Cash digs a little deeper into the drawer and finds something else. He brings it out.

"Clayton gave Michael $10,000," Cash says. He wrote it out here on a receipt." He continues looking at the piece of paper. "The note at the bottom says that it was personal. A favor, I suppose."

"So Michael owed Clayton money?" I ask.

"No," Cash says. "On the receipt it says it was a bonus. So he gave it to him to keep."

"Which means that Clayton wasn't expecting it back," I say.

"Giving him very little motive to make Michael disappear," Cash says. "Especially if he liked the guy well enough to write him a check for $10,000."

I think this over for a moment. And it makes sense. But why did Clayton give Michael $10,000? I voice the question to Cash.

"That's what we need to find out next," Cash says. "But I don't think we're going to find it in Clayton's office." I nod.

"Do you think Michael was in some kind of trouble and needed help to get out of it?" I ask Cash as we put all the papers back and he tucks the letter back into the envelope, sliding it neatly into the drawer.

"That or he had something going on that Clayton was sympathetic to," Cash says. I roll this over in my mind for a moment. Then I think of the infertility treatments.

"Did Michael Berkley have a girlfriend?" I ask. Cash gives me a look. Like that just dawned on him too as a possibility.

"We need to find out," he says.

CHAPTER TWENTY-FIVE

CASH and I spend the rest of the day trying to figure out if Michael Berkley had a girlfriend. I think back to the photo on Instagram. That would make sense. Maybe Clayton had shown Michael that spot– taken him there to talk about things when he was going through such a rough patch–and maybe Michael had liked it so much that he brought someone back there who he thought might enjoy it, too.

But I find nothing on either his Instagram or his Facebook profile. There's really nothing that would point to a romantic connection. There is a woman that he's tagged in a few things, but not for quite some time. Her name is Melanie.

I look at Melanie's profile and I find much the same footprint. There are some things she tagged him in from months ago, but it all tapered off around

September. Which might mean that they were together and they broke up.

Cash is on his computer beside me, looking over the same information I am. Finally, I break the silence.

"So, I'm thinking he and Melanie were involved," I say. Cash looks up from his computer, sitting on the end of my bed.

"That's what I'm gathering, too," Cash says.

"Do you think this could be a case of a crazy ex-girlfriend?" I ask. "Could she have had something to do with his disappearance?"

"Anything's possible," Cash says. "But I don't see a big dramatic trail of posts after they broke up," he goes on. "I would think if she was going to raise hell with him over a breakup, it might start there."

"That's a good point," I tell him. And it is. It certainly seems like if she was the type to try and kill Michael, she'd have made a scene. Even if not on social media, then somewhere that I lot of people would have noticed. And no one has mentioned Melanie.

"How did they meet?" I ask Cash then.

"I'm assuming she was a teacher at the school," he says. "Based on her work history. But she's working somewhere in Oklahoma City now. Not teaching. Working for a non-profit." I nod.

Then that's probably how they met.

"It looks like it was a pretty casual thing, judging from social media," I say. "Maybe they wanted to keep it low profile since they were both working at the high school." Cash seems to think this over. He doesn't say anything for a few moments. "Maybe Clayton was helping him pay off debt. Or legal fees associated with stuff he might have gotten into on the side."

"I don't think Clayton would have just given him the money without a good reason for thinking he needed it. And the guy's got a big heart. I'm thinking that whatever Michael told Clayton he needed it for wasn't what he really need the money for," Cash says.

"I guess we need to talk to Melanie," I say. "Would that be weird?"

"Probably, but it's our only option," Cash says. "And don't discount the fact that Karen saw two other people with her Bigfoot that night. There could be someone involved in this with Melanie."

It seems like things are just getting more and more complicated without either of us being able to come up with a lead that means anything or that might point us in the right direction. The whole thing is starting to feel pointless.

"I think I'm tired of working on this for now," I tell Cash. He sighs and closes his computer.

"Me, too," he says. I stretch my arms over my head. My back hurts from sitting up on the soft surface of the bed with no support.

"We have bigger fish to fry tonight," Cash says with a gleeful smile. And it's contagious.

Clayton and Lisa get back to the house right around the time that Cash and I are heading out to meet up with Katie Reinhart's team. It's dark by the time that Cash's headlights shine across the parking lot in front of the church where the festival is being held. And at the back of the parking lot, I see a group of people and three SUVs. The backs of the SUVs are open and people are shuffling equipment around, all of them bundled up and entirely ready for the weather tonight.

I wore my best coat—the heavier one that I decided I should wear after Cash lent me his jacket—and I'm getting a little too warm in the cab of Cash's truck by the time he pulls into a parking space next to everyone.

I spot Katie in the middle of the group, surely coordinating everything that's going on and everything that's going to transpire later in the evening.

Cash kills the engine and we get out. The two of us walk up to the edge of the commotion and listen for a moment as Katie talks to her team. She lays out a map and glances up, spotting us.

"Blair!" she calls and then she spots Cash. "This must be your friend," she says. She steps around the equipment boxes that the map is resting on and comes up to greet us.

"Cash Kelly," Cash says to Katie. She shakes his hand.

"I've heard about you," Katie says. I watch Cash's face light up at this. It's clear that Katie's a big deal and for her to know who Cash is delights him. "Blair, if I'd known you were bringing him, I'd have hung around for you to introduce us earlier," she says.

Cash gives me an easy smile and puts his arm around me, squeezing my shoulder. I glance at him and smile and when I look back at Katie, there's a smirk on her face. It's there for only a second and she wipes it off quickly, but I blush, knowing what it means. She thinks we're together. And neither of us did anything to correct her.

"Well, let's get to the plan for tonight," she tells us. Then she steps back around to the stack of boxes that hold the map. Someone brings up a flashlight and Cash and I step forward to glean all the information we can about tonight's mission. "Okay, here we are," Katie says, pointing to a position on the map. "And this is where we're going tonight," she points to a location not that far from here. "It's private property but we've been granted access to it for the night. And the guy that owns the place has had several sightings out there. One of them recently. Six weeks ago or so."

I tilt my head to get a better look at the map. It's not far from Clayton's farm, I think. But I can't be entirely certain, not being very familiar with the area at large. Six weeks ago? That was right around the time Michael went missing. I make a mental note about the connection. I'm not sure that it'll prove useful, but at this point I'm taking what I can get. And even though I wanted to keep from thinking about that tonight, I can't help myself.

I sneak a look at Cash and he glances at me. I wonder if he's thinking the same thing. But he looks away quickly, making it hard to judge what's on his mind.

"We're going to break up into a couple of groups. You guys can come with me," Katie says to Cash and myself. "Did you bring any equipment with you or would you like to use some of ours?" she asks. I let Cash field that question.

"We've got a couple of FLIR cameras and a parabolic dish and recorder," Cash says.

"That's great," Katie says, sounding a little bit surprised. I don't imagine she thought I'd be coming out quite so prepared. Sometimes it's a good thing when you make friends with an eccentric monster hunter.

Katie goes on to describe the route we're going to take to get there. The team is all male except for her. And they all listen carefully to what she has to say. It's clear that they respect her a great deal. After that she rolls up the map and Cash and I pile into the SUV with her and a couple of other guys.

"Hi," Cash says to one of them. then to the other, shaking both of their hands. I offer my hand to them and do the same. They're not overly friendly and the level of seriousness on both of their faces has me wondering what we're getting into tonight.

CHAPTER TWENTY-SIX

KATIE DRIVES. She heads out of the parking lot and onto the darkened roadway. The only light comes from the headlights of our vehicle and those behind us. She heads toward the weed farm and we pass it on the way to our destination, making me think that my estimation about the distance between the two locations was correct.

Before long, she turns into a drive that looks a lot like Clayton and Lisa's. It's gravel with overgrown bushes and trees surrounding it. We emerge from the section of foliage and I see a trailer house sitting on a raised foundation in the distance. It has to be a half mile from the road.

By the light of our headlights, I see the surrounding forest that wraps the trailer in an embrace. All of it comes right up to the walls and windows, like the forest is clawing to get inside. It makes the thought that whoever lives here is having experiences with Bigfoot all the more terrifying. The things could be right next to his bedroom window. That is, if they're real.

I can't believe I'm even saying that to myself. Just a month and a half ago I couldn't even admit to myself that my house was possibly haunted. Now, I'm headed out into the middle of nowhere with someone I just met and the person that helped me with the ghost problem.

Life is strange in a fabulous way.

As we pull up to the house, I feel excitement surging in my veins. I'm instantly nervous, wondering what the night will hold. And there's a part of me that wonders if we're going to experience anything. There's a part of me that hopes we will.

I glance over at Cash and offer him a wide grin as we pile out of the car with Katie and the other members of her team. Cash claps his hands together and rubs them, almost too excited to keep it to himself.

Just as we're all getting out of the SUVs and Katie's team is unloading their gear, a voice booms from the house and it seems familiar. I look up at the porch and recognize the man, even in the dim porch light. He stands at least as tall as Cash and he's about twice as wide. It's Linda Stone's nephew. The one who gave us his testimony at the amphitheater the other night.

"Hell, looks like you brought all the troops out," he remarks at the sight of us. Cash goes around to the back of the SUV to help the guys with the equipment and to grab ours. Katie responds to him.

"Thought we could use a solid team to investigate what's been going on out here," she says.

"Well, you know the story inside and out," he says to her. "And the place is yours to traipse around on all night if y'all like," he says. Katie nods.

"Thank you so much for letting us come out here, Nathan," she says.

"No problem," the man says. Katie and the team busy themselves getting their gear out, and Cash does the same. The whole while, Nathan seems to supervise from the porch but says nothing. He watches everyone put on their gear and get their cameras up and running. Then Cash hands me my FLIR and loops the strap attached to his Zoom around his body, carrying the parabolic dish at his waist. I tuck my hand into the strap on the FLIR camera and turn it on, opening the viewing pane so I can get a good look at what the camera is picking up. The heat signatures of everyone in the group light up the screen in red, oranges, and yellows. Nathan is a huge signature in and of himself.

I turn to face Cash and he looks up at me as I stare at him in a series of red, oranges, yellows, greens and blues.

"Don't waste the battery," he says.

"Sorry, captain," I tease him. He jostles my arm playfully.

"I guess we're all ready to go," Katie finally says.

"We're going to go investigate here behind the house first, where Nathan was experiencing the first sightings that he had. We'll break up into two groups and head into the woods. Cash, Blair, you guys come with me and Richard. The rest of you, take the other side and branch off that way," she indicates the opposite direction that we'll be moving in. "Reconvene at the house in four hours."

That'll put us back here at almost midnight, I realize. Hopefully she's not planning on making us spend the entire night out in the woods. I think four hours might be all I can manage. Cash on the other hand looks like he's ready to move in out here.

He's psyched, I can tell. It makes me smile, realizing how important this is to him.

Katie leads the way off to the left side of the house, towards the woods that start just on the other side of it. As we pass by the porch, I realize that Nathan is still standing there, not intending on going with us.

"Is he not coming?" I ask Cash. Cash glances at Nathan and pipes up.

"You not coming out here with us tonight?" he asks the man. The hulking figure turns, his attention now on my companion. He shakes his head.

"I already know what's out there, and my thought on the whole thing is better you than me," he says simply. There's something dark in his tone, though. I feel a chill that has nothing to do with the frigid temperatures tonight. It has everything to do with how

Nathan said that. This huge man is scared to go into the woods behind his own home. He believes something truly is out there. And here I am, trying to find out for myself.

But Cash seems unphased and continues walking, following the group. I hang back for a moment, and look at Nathan. I see his eyes watching me in the darkness. After a moment, it makes me uncomfortable enough that I double my walking speed to catch up to the group.

"Thought we lost you back there," Cash teases as we enter the forest, cracking branches and shuffling through leaves, stepping over fallen pieces of tree trunk, and generally trying to keep up with Katie, who leads the way as if this is the most natural, easiest thing in the world.

I find myself already breathing harder than I'd like after about five minutes of heading into the woods. I don't imagine that Katie or any of her team have this problem because I can't hear any of them breathing ahead of us.

Finally, after about fifteen minutes of walking, we arrive at a clearing. Though unlike the one where we found the lanyard, this one is flat ground. No ridge to look over. The trees surround us, encroaching ominously on our little troupe.

I glance around, the darkness something that my eyes have made their best attempt to adjust to. But I still wonder what's out here. Even if there isn't a

Sasquatch, there's probably something equally, if not more scary. Like bears. Or people. The thought of meeting either out here tonight is enough to send another chill down my spine.

Suddenly, I'm wondering what exactly I was thinking when I accepted Katie's offer. I'm a city girl. This isn't the way that I'm supposed to pass my time. I get freaked out by the densely wooded area that lines my own property and have no desire to go check it out.

I feel myself starting to panic as everyone gathers in the clearing. Cash turns to me, apparently hearing my heavy breathing. Now, it's not a result of exertion, but of what's going on inside my head. I feel like the woods around us are closing in. Like I can see the forest moving, breathing. A living monster that exists only to swallow us up.

My breathing becomes more rapid, shallower. C ash places a hand on my shoulder. He stoops slightly, looking into my eyes.

"Are you okay?" he asks quietly. I shake my head fervently, no. But I say nothing. "It's okay," he assures me. "I'm going to be with you the whole time," he says. He squeezes my shoulder and reaches into his jacket pocket. He fishes something out and hands me one of the super sour candies that he gave me at my house when I had a panic attack in front of him once before. I tear the wrapper manically and pop it into my mouth as Katie begins to direct everyone. Cash takes the lead, listening to her instructions and keeping one eye on me, making sure that I'm okay.

I feel my heart rate slowing down. Feel myself becoming more grounded. I ask Cash for a bottle of water, and he pulls one out of his pack and hands it to me. I gulp it greedily and feel the panic that swelled in my chest only moments before begin to dissipate. Now, it's time to do what I came out here to do.

"Alright," Katie says, seemingly none the wiser to my little moment of hysteria, though her gaze does linger on me as I finish off the bottle of water right then and there, handing the empty container back to Cash. "Everyone ready?" she asks. "Cash, you and Blair come with me," she says. "Guys, take that other side of the clearing to the west." The other two guys with us nod.

Katie comes walking over to us and my anxiety is replaced with something else, maybe eagerness. The wave of fear subsides and a sense of adventure takes its place. I survived my little panic attack. I can do this.

And then Katie asks us, "Are you guys ready to hunt some Bigfoot?"

CHAPTER TWENTY-SEVEN

KATIE LEADS us to the eastern side of the clearing, and once again, we're swallowed by the forest that surrounds us. This time, though, I feel more at ease. I'm sandwiched between Katie and Cash, with Cash bringing up the rear hot on my heels. He seems intent on keeping his promise that he won't let me out of his sight.

I glance back at him. He carries the FLIR camera in one hand and the parabolic dish in the other, scanning the horizon with both, it case he spots something. In front of me, Katie has a FLIR camera, too. She listens intently to our surroundings, turning her head this way and that with each unexpected sound that greets us in the woods. She too scans the forest for some sign of something. I follow suit, looking for any kind of heat signature. And it's then that I spot something.

"Hey!" I whisper. The two of them stop and come to my side. "I see something." Off to the right, there's a heat signature. A smallish animal, foraging at the base of a tree slipping in and out of the bushes that surround it.

"Good eyes," Katie says. "A raccoon, I think."

The three of us watch the little guy for a while. Finally, Katie directs us to follow her, apparently satisfied with her raccoon encounter for the evening. I keep scanning our surroundings for something bigger, part of me wondering just how common bears are out here. It looks like prime bear habitat. I wonder if anyone gets killed by bears in these woods. A sudden desire to know the statistics on that strikes me. But out here, my signal is zilch. I couldn't find out if I wanted to.

I focus my attention back on the path ahead of us. The path that Katie is cutting at the front of our little procession.

"Stop," Cash says. Both of us turn to face him, stopping instantly. He's pointing the parabolic dish out to the west and holding his FLIR camera with the other. He points it in the same direction and Katie and I follow suit, doing the same. "Can you guys hear that?" he asks.

We grow silent, not moving amongst the foliage. I strain my ears and in the distance, I make out something faint. The sound of an animal call, though it's so far away that I have trouble doing anything other than knowing it's there.

"Yes," Katie says.

"Listen ," Cash says, handing her his headphones. She steps around and takes them from him, placing them over her ears. I look from them back in the direction that Cash heard something, utterly helpless without the help of the headphones.

Suddenly, I feel naked. Like I'm exposed on every side. Like whatever is out there might approach at any second, taking advantage of my vulnerability. I almost hold my breath, realizing after about thirty seconds that I'm not breathing.

Katie listens intently on the headphones. A smile breaks across her face when I look back at her, hoping she'll say something.

"They're talking to each other," she tells Cash. "Here," she says, looking at me and handing over the headphones. I slip them on and listen.

As they go over my ears, the sounds of the forest are instantly amplified. I hear bugs and birds and small foraging creatures, but then I hear something else that makes the hair on the back of my neck stand up. A cry that is neither human nor animal. There's emotion in it. A high keening sound, like a howl and a scream mixed together.

My heart races.

And then I hear another howling scream answer the first call. My eyes widen and I look at Cash. He grins wide in the moonlit forest and I feel something like awe fill my chest. My eyes water slightly at the thought of what I might be hearing. It's an incredible experience. Spiritual, almost.

The howl is clearly not a coyote. I have those at my house and I know the sounds they make. It's also not a person, or people. No person could make a sound like this.

I glance over at Katie and slip the headphones off, seeing that she wants to tell me something.

"You just heard a Sasquatch," she says to me with glee in her voice. "I'm not sure you realize how fortu-nate that is. Most people don't get to hear or see one on their first trip out into the woods," she adds, then points at Cash. "He might be your lucky charm, Blair."

I look back at Cash and smile at him. And I swear he's blushing in the moonlight. And with that, we continue in the direction of the howls, hoping that we'll actually get to see something tonight, and not just hear them.

We never get close enough to get a heat signature on the FLIR cameras. Unfortunately. I feel a heady giddiness following me out of the woods. I went from being petrified at the idea to understanding why so many people love to spend time out there. Hearing that noise—the call—was something else.

In a bittersweet moment, I wish that I could call my dad and tell him about it. What would he make of something like that?

Even though I know he did all he could to expose Holloway as a hoaxer, I wonder what his personal opinion on Bigfoot really was. For the first time in my adult life, I have the urge to go through his papers. To really dig into the records he left behind. I wonder what I might find. These ideas are circulating around in my brain as we emerge out of the woods a few hours later, showing up back at Nathan's trailer house.

As we round the corner of the house and start packing equipment back up into the truck, Katie stops to talk to us.

"I hope that you guys had a good time tonight," she says with a smile. "That audio you caught was great, Cash," she adds. "I'd love a copy of that recording if you don't mind."

"Of course ," Cash says.

"I had an amazing time," I tell Katie. "That was wonderful."

"Likewise," Cash says to her and we shake hands. The three of us load up our stuff into the SUV and shortly afterwards the guys on the other team and the guys that we split with show back up in front of Nathan's trailer house.

Apparently, because of the commotion we make sharing our evidence, Nathan comes back out onto the porch.

"Y'all find anything out there?" he asks. Katie goes over the evidence with Nathan and he seems interested in it, but when they're done, he clears his throat. "Well, I'm grateful to y'all for coming out here," he says. "You're welcome back all week or anytime that you want to come on down. I don't think these critters are going anywhere."

"Thank you so much for your hospitality," Katie says.

"That all being said, there is something I think I should mention," Nathan says. The group of us look up at him, pausing in the midst of our conversations. "You better get over to the weed farm," he says. "I just got a phone call that Harrison Holloway just shot a Bigfoot."

CHAPTER TWENTY-EIGHT

"WHAT?" Cash asks.

When I look over at him, confusion colors his features. Katie looks much the same. There's a murmur that goes through the group of us.

"That's what I just got a call about from a friend of mine. He sounded worked up. But if I were y'all, I'd go check it out. In fact, I'm about to get in my pickup and head over there."

I look at Cash, my eyes wide.

Everyone on the team piles into the two vehicles we brought over here. Katie doesn't bother stopping back by the church to let Cash and I get our truck. She plows forward, gravel ricocheting off the body of her SUV and surely hitting the guys behind us. She hauls ass for the weed farm.

On squealing tires we come to a screeching halt not too far from the place where Harrison Holloway gave his performance the other night. Except this time, people are crowding around the edge of the woods, blocking any view we might have of what's going on inside. Katie kills the engine and the six of us pile out, heading immediately for the commotion.

"What's going on?" she demands of the first person that turns to look at her.

"Holloway shot something," he stammers.

Katie's face grows dark, suspecting what I'm hoping isn't the case. But an uneasiness settles in my stomach. I glance at Cash, hoping he'll give me some unspoken sign that will alleviate it. But he doesn't. His face is just as hard as hers, expecting the worst.

"Call 911!" someone shouts as the crowd begins to part. A guy beside us fumbles for his phone.

"I got it," Cash says, grabbing his own cell and keying in the emergency number quickly. I hold my breath as the crowd continues to widen its ranks, allowing someone through. Cash steps off to the side and I hear him talking to the operator.

"He's been shot!" someone else yells, and finally the crowd breaks.

Holloway takes front and center as a man lays bleeding on the ground, his fellow Bigfooters at his side, having carried him out of the woods.

"No reason to panic!" Holloway says in a tone that's far too confident for what's happening. Panicking seems like the only reasonable response to me. And a number of people seem to be doing just that. And as he continues to speak–digging himself a hole–the crowd begins to turn on him.

"You shot him!" someone yells at Holloway. A roar rips through the crowd and I can't make out what Cash is saying to the operator anymore. The last thing I heard was that he told her someone was shot, relaying the information given by the parting crowd.

I stoop to the ground, going to the man's side.

"Are you alright?" I ask.

He looks at me like I'm crazy, which feels like a good sign. He's emotional and pissed off. At least he hasn't lost so much blood that a reaction like that would be impossible.

"Do I look alright to you, lady?" he demands of me. He's been shot in the leg, but it doesn't look like it clipped his artery. There's not enough blood for that. Still, someone put a tourniquet on him, slowing down what bleeding there is.

Cash steps back over beside me, having gotten off the phone.

Holloway tries to calm the crowd.

"Everything's fine, folks," he says in a placating tone.

"The hell it is," the guy on the ground says.

"The police and the EMTs are on their way," Cash says. "No telling when they'll get here, though."

He faces Holloway. People are shouting epithets at Holloway and the crowd is growing restless. He tries once again to calm them, but Cash cuts him off.

"I think it's time for you to shut up and sit down," Cash says gruffly, his tone more aggressive than I've ever heard it.

"You don't know shit, son," Holloway says.

"I know you're a fraud and now you've shot someone," Cash counters.

"Like I said," Holloway growls. "You don't know shit."

Katie comes back to where we are and she looks at Holloway.

"You almost killed someone tonight," she tells him, getting up in his face. Katie isn't much taller than me, and for a moment I fear for her safety. Holloway bows up to her, like he's not afraid to hit a woman. Cash steps between them.

"You wanna fight with somebody tonight, why don't you fight with me," Cash says.

"Cash!" I hiss, not wanting this to devolve into violence, but sensing that it could at any moment.

The crowd is growing more hostile, murmurs rippling through it about Holloway being a fraud and a hoax. A joke within the community. He looks around himself, feeling the crowd turning on him. The people that came out here tonight to see what he had to offer in the way of evidence and entertainment are now becoming his enemies. But Holloway doesn't seem willing to give it all up quite yet.

"You all know what you saw out here tonight!" he yells across the crowd, trying to summon them back to his side. They quiet just enough to be able to hear what the man has to say. "You all saw the creature out there tonight," he shouts, his voice commanding attention. He's a real Jim Jones type. "I had him in my sights and I pulled the trigger," he says. "The forest was dark and my friend here must have stepped into the line of fire."

"You're not the victim here, Holloway," Katie pipes up. "And you never were the victim of anything but your own poor choices," she adds. "You're a disgrace to the Bigfoot community and you know it. This shit with Karen Dunham is just you trying desperately to make yourself relevant again so you can scam someone else."

Even in the moonlight, I see the rage bubbling below Holloway's surface. He clenches his fists at his side and his jaw tenses. His nostrils flare slightly. An assault on his ego, he can't take.

"I've done more for this community than you ever will, little girl," he says to her, demeaning her position with the university. She isn't phased, probably used to misogyny in her day-to-day life as a woman in the anthropology department at a major university. I feel a swell of pride for her. For the fact that she asked me to join her tonight.

"You'll get yours, Holloway," she says. And I wonder immediately if the guy he shot is going to press charges. Judging from the way he's acting, I would think he is. I hope he will.

I stand up next to Cash and Holloway spots me.

"You," he points a finger at me and says the word as if it's the worst insult he could hurl at me.

"She has nothing to do with this," Cash says to Holloway. "It's just your bad luck that you should have hard feelings for someone who was practically a child when you were exposed as a fraud, Holloway."

"Your dad always had to stick his nose where it didn't belong," Holloway tells me, his eyes never bothering to leave mine. "And it looks like it runs in the family," he says. But before Holloway can say much more, I hear the sounds of a siren in the distance. The EMTs. The police.

Holloway looks off to our right, where the noises are coming from. Then he glances down at the man he shot, and for a second I think I see a flicker of fear run across his face. He's scared the guy might press charges. I want to tell him, *good, you should be. You shot the guy for Christ's sake.* But I don't.

Cash reaches out for me and pulls me in, wrapping his arm over my shoulder, and he leads me off to the far side of the road, away from where everyone is gathered.

"Are you okay?" he asks.

"Stop asking me that," I say with a little bite. "I'm not fine china. I'm not going to break into a million little pieces at the first sign of conflict, Cash," I say. But instantly I regret it, seeing the hurt on his face. He's just looking out for me. I apologize. "Sorry, this is just weird."

"Not quite what you imagined when I asked you if

you wanted to go out of town for the weekend, is it?" he asks with a smile. He kicks some gravel on the ground and looks around us. "Sure as hell isn't what I imagined the weekend would be," he remarks. It comes out softly, almost like he's speaking to himself. It makes me smile.

"It's fine," I tell him. "Besides," I say. "What else would I be doing this weekend if not trying to unravel a Bigfoot hoax?" He laughs.

"I can think of quite a few things that might be more fun than this," Cash says good-naturedly. "But alas, here we are."

"It's not so bad," I tell him. His eyes come back to me.

"We're even going to be back at the house before two in the morning tonight," he adds with a laugh.

"This is true," I say. But the frivolity of our conversation, surely engineered by Cash to take my mind off of the seriousness of the situation, is cut short when a set of red and blue lights come tearing up the road. The police are here. And so is the ambulance.

CHAPTER TWENTY-NINE

TWO OFFICERS GET out of the police car and
several EMTs climb out of the back of the ambulance,
all of them heading straight for the man bleeding on
the ground. The crowd gives them a wide berth.

"Now, officers," Holloway starts to say to one of
them. He cuts him off with a gesture of his hand.

"We'll talk later," the officer says. Holloway looks
affronted, as if he can't imagine a world in which his
own testimony is more important than that of the man
he shot and almost killed. It's astounding, the ego on
the man.

Cash and I stay where we are, and Katie comes
over to join us. I spot Nathan on the other side of the
crowd, watching the EMTs begin their work on the
injured man. The police talk to him briefly, getting an
initial statement from him in which he points, very
animatedly at Harrison Holloway.

I cast a glance over at Holloway and see that he's swallowing hard, a lump bobbing in his throat. I hope he's sweating it as much as possible.

Holloway is a con man, so he's probably used to being in a scrape. But I don't know if he's used to being in one quite like this.

I hear people murmuring behind us, talking about the shooting. One of them speculates that if Holloway can't tell the difference between a tall guy and a Bigfoot, that he's probably never seen a Bigfoot in his life. The other one agrees with this, saying that Holloway is for sure a fraud. The interactions around the perimeter of the crowd are much the same, everyone agreeing that Holloway is in over his depth and likely doesn't know what the fuck he's doing.

"I could have told them that," Katie mumbles under her breath, obviously doing her best to listen in on their conversations as I am.

"Have you dealt with him a lot?" I ask her.

"Far more than I'd care to," Katie admits. "The guy was always starting shit back in the day. Back when your dad took care of him. Or at least we thought he had. Must be that reptiles have nine lives just like cats," she adds. Cash snorts at this.

"It certainly seems that way," I say to Katie. For a moment, I think of Noelle's cousin, Jenna, and how she's probably the biggest reptile I've ever known. Jenna most certainly is the type to keep coming back like a bad rash. Holloway doesn't seem much different in my eyes. Both of them are the type to suck the life out of people, just to get what they want. Anyone is a means to an end to people like them. It makes me worry for Noelle, with Jenna getting out of prison this year.

The EMTs get the man who was shot loaded onto a stretcher and start wheeling him back to the ambulance. The police then turn their attention to Holloway and the crowd. They question him and start asking questions of people standing around, trying to get those that saw the events unfold to give their statements first.

"I imagine it's not every day that a police officer has to take a bunch of statements about how a guy shot another guy, thinking he was Bigfoot," Cash remarks. I look at him and chuckle, grateful for his way of lightening the mood at even the darkest times.

Finally, the officers take a statement from Katie, who tells them that the three of us really weren't there for the shooting. That we came over when we assumed the worst had happened after getting news that Holloway had shot Bigfoot. They thank us for our statement and I glance over, seeing that a couple of officers are still raking Holloway over the coals, likely unsatisfied with his version of events. I can only imagine that it's far more colorful and full of intriguing than the way things actually went down.

The three of us stand there for a few more moments and Katie thanks us again for coming out with her and her team, even if the night ended in a less fun way than it started.

"Thank you for the experience," I tell her. And I mean it. It seems like days ago now, hearing those creatures in the woods. I'm glad Cash has the recording. He agrees once again to send that to Katie the second he gets it onto his computer. She tells him that she wants to use it at the next conference she speaks at. We're managing to make pleasant conversation when the officers break up the crowd.

"Alright, folks," one of the officers says. "Enough chit chat. Things are over here for tonight. Nothing else to see, so go on home. We'll be in touch if we have any further questions."

"I guess that's our cue," Cash says. And Katie turns to go back to the SUV. Just as she gets a few steps ahead of us, Holloway steps up to Cash, cutting him off and forcing him to stop in his tracks. I turn around to face the two of them.

"I know what you're about," Holloway says to Cash. "And your little girlfriend. Both of you don't know when to keep your nose out of someone else's business," he goes on. There's an angry fire in his eyes that has nothing to do with the moonlight. It's chilling. Holloway confirmed tonight that he would hurt anyone if he thought it could further his agenda. And I don't want that to befall me and Cash.

"Listen up," Cash says to Holloway, leaning toward the finger he has poking into Cash's chest. Cash presses forward so hard that Holloway's face is inches from his own when he speaks. "I will do everything in my power to expose you for who you are," Cash says. "Just like Graham did. You can count on that, Holloway. You take advantage of people and I hate that, understand?"

Holloway scoffs, but there's a nervousness to it. Cash's imposing figure bearing down on him probably has something to do with that. Cash leans in some more. "It's not going to seem funny when you have to find a new grift," he tells Holloway. And then he leans back.

"Come on," Cash says to me as he approaches. But Holloway has one last thing to say.

"You shouldn't listen to him, girl," he says. "You'll end up like your old man." I stop in my tracks and turn to face Holloway. the words cut too deep. They're too personal. I want to spit in Holloway's face. "Like I said, he was always sticking his nose where it didn't belong and I think that's what finally got him in the end," Holloway says.

My heart beats faster, blood thundering in my ears. I don't want him to talk about my dad. Not like that. Not at all. He doesn't deserve to. I start to head back towards Holloway, hellbent on hitting him in the jaw so hard he needs false teeth. But Cash stops me.

He wraps his arms around me from behind and pulls me close. I can feel tears burning at the edges of my eyes. I want at Holloway so bad that I think about elbowing Cash in the gut. I don't, though. It's too late, though, because Holloway knows he got to me. He laughs, big and deep. The sound filling the area around us, swallowing me up like I'm a defenseless little girl.

I turn with Cash and we start to head back to the truck, but I hear Holloway's laughter all the way there.

"He's a fucking prick," Cash offers as consolation. But it's not enough.

"I want to ruin him," I tell Cash. I say it with conviction. With passion. And with truth. I want Holloway to have a hard time ever finding work again. I never want him to be able to take advantage of anyone the way he took advantage of people back in the day or the way he's done it to Karen Dunham. My heart is racing by the time we get into Katie's SUV. And I'm grateful that she turns on the radio for background noise on the way back to the church. I'm not sure I could stomach talking about all of it right now.

Holloway's words echo in my mind. His dark laughter. The way it gave him pleasure to see me so angry. He's worse than a conman. He's evil. And tonight he proved just how far he was willing to go for his con. He almost killed someone, and he'd likely do it again. There was no remorse in his eyes. He saw himself as the victim. As we drive back I press my face against the cold, black window beside me, and I vow that I'm going to do everything in my power to put and end to Harrison Holloway.

CHAPTER THIRTY

"THANKS AGAIN," Cash says as we load up the last of our stuff from Katie's SUV. The team waves at us and Cash and I climb into the cab of his truck.

It's bitter cold inside the vehicle and I blow on my hands to warm them up. Cash starts it and the engine rumbles to life. I'm eager for some of the air blowing off of it to warm up to, though I'm not sure that will happen before we arrive back at Clayton and Lisa's.

"I take it you're going to have a lot to tell your friend," I tease Cash, trying to sound like I'm in a good mood. But Holloway's threats are weighing on me. I hate the way he talked about my dad. Like he had some right to talk about him like that when he absolutely doesn't.

"I guess so," Cash says with a little chuckle. "Clayton's not gonna believe this shit. Or actually, he might," Cash says. We drive down the road a little ways and

Cash lets me have my silence. He doesn't bother turning on the radio or anything, and I'm grateful to him for that. When we pull into the driveway, the truck is finally getting warm, and Cash kills the engine. It's then that he speaks.

"I'm sorry about what happened back there," he says to me in the darkness of the pickup cab. I unbuckle my seatbelt, the only sound between us.

"It's not your fault," I assure him. It isn't. This probably would have happened with or without Cash. In fact, I'm sure of it.

"Still," Cash says.

"That guy would have had it out for me even without you egging him on," I tell him.

"Yeah, but you wouldn't be in this position if I hadn't brought you down here," he says.

"Do you regret it?" I ask him.

"Of course not," he says. He looks over at me in the darkened cab, our faces only illuminated by the moonlight outside. "I'm glad you're here with me, Blair," he says. I feel myself blushing all the way up my face from my collarbone. In the darkness, Cash reaches for my hand and I give it to him. His palm is warm, dry, and swallows my small hand up. I look at our hands there together for a moment in the moonlight. For a brief second, I don't want it to end. I want him to keep holding my hand. But we can't stay out here forever. Eager to keep this moment going, I suggest something.

"Why don't we have a beer when we get inside?" I ask.

"I could use one," he says with a laugh. And the two of us get out of the truck and head up to the house. Cash unlocks the door with the spare key and we enter as quietly as we can. I sneak over to the fridge and it sounds like everyone's asleep. I open it up and grab two beers and pop the caps off of them. I hand one to Cash.

"Want to sit where we sat the other night?" he asks me. I'm in my warmest coat and with the fire pit and the windscreen, the patio isn't too cold. I nod. He stops in his tracks as I follow him out the back door. I hear music and the sound of the fire going and I step out from behind Cash. Clayton turns, beer in hand, and several empties sitting on the edge of the fire pit. He greets us warmly.

"There you two are!" he says, wrapping both of us in a hug. "Come, sit down," he says.

"Hey, man," Cash says, wrapping him in a hug with me squeezed in on the other side. "What are you doing out here?" Cash asks, taking a seat on the outside edge of the patio enclosure. He leaves me the warmest seat, near the corner.

"Lisa and I are fighting," he says. "I wasn't quite ready to hang my head and go curl up on the couch yet." He smiles at both of us and raises his glass. "To better times ahead," he says. Cash and I toast him and Clayton turns the music up slightly. "This is the song that we danced to at our wedding," he tells me. It's a country number. Something red dirt and I recognize the singer. A guy from Oklahoma that got into a bunch of controversy after a shooting at one of his concerts. I nod and smile. The song is wonderful. And I can certainly imagine someone dancing to it at their wedding.

"It'll be alright," Cash says.

"I know," Clayton says. "It's about money," he adds. "Ain't it always?" he chuckles. "I spent too much of it and now it's tight. So she's mad at me and she's got every right to be." I chance a furtive glance at Cash, thinking about the receipt we saw for the $10,000 that Clayton gave to Michael.

Clayton slurs his words a little, obviously quite tipsy and nearly drunk. And he doesn't catch what goes between Cash and me unspoken. Cash seizes the opportunity, though.

"What have you been spending so much money on, man?" he asks him.

"Trying to help a friend a month ago," Clayton admits. I sit up straighter in my seat, eager for what he's going to say next. Maybe with him drunk, he'll have loose lips and tell us more than we already know.

"Lending money to friends ends nowhere good," Cash says, then takes a sip of his beer. His eyes meet mine briefly, then he looks back at Clayton. Clayton rubs his face and takes his cap off, rubbing his head before replacing the hat.

"Well, I didn't lend it," Clayton says. "But it still didn't work out."

"You gave someone money?" I ask, trying to sound as innocent as possible. "I'm sure you had a good reason, then."

"I thought I did," Clayton admits. "I gave money to that guy, the missing one. Michael," he says. "Ten grand. He said he and his girlfriend were about to have to look into fertility treatments. I felt for him, you know," Clayton says. I know, indeed. Cash pushes him with the questioning.

"I guess he never got to use it," Cash says.

"I think he ran off with it, man," Clayton says. "Which makes me feel even dumber for giving it to him. I think he and his old lady broke up right before Michael went missing. And I don't think he's all that missing, if you get my drift."

"That hurts, man," Cash says. He whistles. "So you gave him that money, thinking he would use it for fertility treatments for her?"

"Exactly," Clayton says. "I think he played me. Maybe he was in some kind of trouble. Or some kind of debt that he needed to pay off quick. There ain't no telling. Especially now," he adds. Cash clears his throat.

"I meant to tell you that the other day, we went up to that ridge where you and I used to hang out," Cash says. A smile breaks across Clayton's face.

"Oh, yeah?" he asks.

"Yeah, and we found some stuff that I've been meaning to ask you about. Michael's lanyard was up there along with his planner from the school," Cash says gingerly. I can tell it's hard for him, telling his friend these things. Asking the questions that he has to ask.

"Did you?" Clayton asks, unphased. "I guess he must have gone back up there after I took him there. That's where we talked about the money he needed. But I didn't see any lanyard or planner on him. He only had that stuff when he was teaching, I think." Cash seems to breathe a sigh of relief. Clayton narrows his eyes and a goofy smile breaks across his face.

"Wait a fucking minute?" Clayton says, laughter in his voice. "You didn't think I did something to Michael, did you?" Cash struggles to find the right words. "Oh, my God, you did," Clayton laughs. "I should have done something to him when he disappeared with that fucking money," he adds, his tone joking. I look at Cash with a smile and shrug. "You should probably call the cops about that shit you found," Clayton says. "Call them now," he adds. "They'll send someone out to get it, I bet." Cash laughs. He sounds relieved.

"You're right," Cash says. "I'll call. Do either of you want another beer?" Cash asks, standing up and preparing to go make his call to the police.

"I'll take one," Clayton says and I shake my head,

telling Cash I'm fine. "I'll be right back," Cash says, indicating that he's going inside. And he leaves Clayton and I to our own devices while he makes a call to the sheriff's department and grabs another beer for Clayton.

CHAPTER THIRTY-ONE

I'M quiet for a few moments, unsure how to fill the silence between Clayton and myself. I barely know him and I feel like I was just made privy to information that he might not have told me if he hadn't been drunk. It makes me unsure of how to proceed conversationally from here. But it doesn't take him long after that to fill the silence, and I'm grateful for the sound of his voice filling the silence when he begins to speak.

"Cash is lucky to have you, Blair," he says. Instantly I'm not sure if I'd have rather he'd just have stayed quiet. Maybe sometimes silence is better, I think, unsure of where he's going with this. But I can't deny that my heart is beating faster for the third time tonight, and it has nothing to do with Bigfoot or Harrison Holloway. I'm eager to see what Clayton has to say.

"I don't know if I'd say that," I tell him. But I smile

to myself, looking down at the fire dancing in front of us.

"He hasn't had anyone in a long time," Clayton goes on. I shift nervously in my seat, a little terrified that at any moment, Cash could walk out here and hear us talking about this. I wonder how he'd feel. I'm still trying to gauge how I feel talking about it all.

"We're not exactly...together," I tell Clayton. Clayton laughs.

"I've known that fool for a long time, sister," he says. "And I know what that look he gets around you means. Don't break his heart too badly." But before I can ask Clayton anything else on the subject, Cash comes out the back door, tucking his phone into his pocket and two beers held in his other hand.

"What did I miss?" Cash asks. I look nervously at Clayton, but his question must be rhetorical, because he goes on. "Cops should be here in a little while. Said they were happy to take a look at what we found. I didn't bother mentioning that we found it a few days ago and I gave my friend the chance to tell me if he was a murderer," he says to Clayton, nudging his arm and Clayton takes one of the beers in Cash's hand.

Cash sits down and finishes off the beer he had out here from earlier. Then he starts nursing this new one. I realize I've still got a half a bottle left and drink up.

The three of us pass the time like that, talking about easy subjects until a cop car pulls up out front.

Clayton gets up and Cash and I do the same, all of us leaving our beer bottles here on the back patio. Then we walk through the house and meet the cop on the front porch. Before we do, Cash runs up to his room and grabs the planner and the lanyard. He meets us at the bottom of the stairs and we all go outside to greet the officer.

He's a young guy, and I recognize him instantly from earlier. He was one of the officers trying to get Holloway to give them a statement. And I'm sure Holloway did. One in which he's not the perpetrator at all, but the victim.

"Good evening," he says to the three of us. "I hear y'all have some stuff that we might want to see concerning the Michael Berkley disappearance," he says.

"That's right," Cash says. "Here you go. He hands the two items to the officer but the planner drops. When it hits the ground, it's dried out enough, apparently from the warmth of the house, that the front opens up to the place where it invited someone to write their name. Whoever might have possessed it. But when I look at the name as I stoop to scoop it up, I see that it's not Michael's name.

Instead, it bears Haley Stone's name, phone number, and address.

I say nothing, instead opting to listen. I'll tell them about that when he leaves. "The pages are real stuck together," Cash tells him about the planner. If you could get it all the way dried out, you might be able to tell something about what's inside," he says.

"There's a lab in OKC that can do that for us," the officer says. "I appreciate y'all handing in this stuff," he goes on. "We're looking for some kind of break and it hasn't been easy coming across it. This might have something we can use. So you found Michael's lanyard with the planner?"

"Yes," Cash says. "Up on that ridge that overlooks the valley," he says, as if anyone from the area would immediately know exactly where he was talking about.

"Well, thank you all," the officer says. And he tips his hat to me and then turns around to head down the steps back out to his cruiser.

"Let's go finish our beers," Clayton says. And the three of us head into the house and out onto the back patio. Clayton turns the music up a little more. Loudly enough that I become slightly concerned that Lisa is going to pop her head out the door at any moment and tell him to shut it off, but that doesn't happen. Instead, Clayton and Cash start combing through their memories of better times. Times they shared back in the day, and I listen.

The two of them attended high school together. In fact, Lisa went to the same school. She and Clayton have been together since way back then. They tell me about some nights they spent out at the lake trying to stargaze and all they caught in their telescope was skinny-dipping college kids.

After several more stories like that, Clayton finally stands up and excuses himself.

"Well," he says. "I've sure had a lot of fun with the two of you, but if I'm not up early making breakfast, I think Lisa might file for divorce. And I can't have that," he teases.

"Goodnight," I tell him. Cash echoes my sentiment. And the two of us remain seated next to each other on the love seat against the wall in front of the fire pit. Clayton closes the door behind him and I hear him stirring around in the kitchen for a little bit. Finally, the lights in the house on the bottom floor go out and I assume that he's found himself a comfortable spot on the couch where he can sleep.

The fire crackles in front of us, the flames dancing high then sweeping low, and creating all sorts of shapes as they burn in the night. I stare at it, then hold my hands out to it, seeking its warmth. I think about why I wanted to come back here with Cash in the first place. But I think the moment is gone. Interrupted by Clayton. But that's okay. Being out here with Cash is nice, at any rate, in whatever capacity. Finally, I speak.

"I think we need to get a hold of Michael's girlfriend," I say.

"I think you're right," Cash says in response.

"It's just too weird that they broke up and then he went missing, along with Clayton's ten grand," I say.

"What if she has something to do with him going missing?" I ask.

"That very well could be," Cash says. "I'm not discounting that."

"I'll do what I can to try and figure out how to get a hold of her tomorrow," I tell Cash. "Oh," I add. "I noticed something when the planner popped open."

"What's that?" he asks.

"Well, it wasn't Michael's planner," I say. "It was Haley Stone's."

"The girl who was on his cross country team?" Cash asks.

"That very one," I say.

"Hmm," Cash says, seeming to think about this. "Why would her stuff have been out there? Could he have told her that he was planning on disappearing? They were close, after all."

"That's sort of what I'm wondering," I say to Cash. Then I sit back against the loveseat. His arm is stretched out behind me. As I settle back into my seat, I feel the warmth of his arm against my neck, even through his jacket. The two of us stay there, for a long time. Neither of us saying anything. Neither of us moving. Maybe it's just my imagination. Or wishful thinking. But I could swear that it's because neither of us want to move. Neither of us want the moment to end. I can't tell you how I know that, but I can feel it somewhere deep down inside my gut. And it fills me with warmth.

CHAPTER THIRTY-TWO

THE NEXT MORNING, I have only one mission in mind. I want to talk to Holly about Haley Stone. And over coffee, I float the idea with Cash. Clayton is in the kitchen, letting Lisa sleep in as he makes our breakfast. Surely earning some brownie points after his night on the couch. Cash stirs his coffee after putting some creamer and sugar into it.

"Sometimes you need it sweet," he remarks. I smile and think about him guzzling coffee black after our first night down here. He's a lot of things, but a morning person isn't one of them. I decide to broach the subject anyway, whether he's all the way awake. We still have a way to go to figure out what's going on in Hobby Hollow. I never realized that I could be such a busy-body, but here we are. And I have to admit that it's a little fun.

"I think we need to talk to Holly," I tell Cash. The

sound of bacon sizzling sets the backdrop to our conversation. Clayton curses, apparently having burned himself on some grease.

"Where can we find her?" Cash asks. Overhearing our conversation, Clayton speaks up after nursing his burn.

"She'll probably be at the festival today," he says. "You could catch up with her there." It sounds like an ambush when he puts it that way. And though that's not the way I intend it, I want to ask Holly about Haley in a non-threatening atmosphere. It makes it sound sinister. But we need the information. I want to know what Michael Berkley's relationship was to Haley, because I'm fairly certain that she was his favorite student. And maybe Michael told her something about where he might have been going.

"I imagine if Haley knows anything, she's kept it to herself," I say.

"I would bet you're right," Cash replies. "If he was her mentor and her favorite teacher, she probably feels a good amount of loyalty to the guy."

He's right, she probably does. No matter why Michael disappeared, if she shared that with a teenager that thought the world of him, she isn't going to spill the beans that easily.

Finally, Lisa joins us and Clayton serves breakfast. The four of us eat, making pleasant conversation and Lisa seems to be in a better mood just because Clayton fed us. I don't blame her. I think often, so much of what happens within the walls of a household falls to the wife or the woman, and men don't give it much of a second thought. In so many ways, we've come worlds from the time when women couldn't vote. And in others, we're still stuck in a time warp.

My focus has been on my breakfast, and I look up across the table at Cash. And I catch him staring at me. He looks away quickly and I can't help but think about what Clayton said last night. I glance over at Clayton and find him looking back and forth between the two of us as Lisa's saying something about her flowerbeds and the spring. He smirks and I look down, intent on finishing my breakfast with nothing embarrassing happening.

After breakfast, Cash and I get ready to head over to the festival. Clayton tells us to have a good time and I imagine he's spending the time with Lisa to continue to smooth things over.

"Smart man," Cash remarks as he slips into his coat. I shrug on my jacket and nod.

"Very," I say with a smirk.

Cash and I head out the door and get into his truck. He turns the engine over and we head for the main road. Once we're out there, he turns on some music and we pass the time without talking, but it's comfortable. There's something easy about the silence with him. Even without music, I feel at home. Like I don't have to fill it like I do with so many people. The only other person I really know that offers me that is Noelle.

It's something special. Not to be overlooked, I think. Not all relationships are like that. And that leads me to another thought.

Changing our relationship to anything other than what it is right now might lead us to a place where that companionable silence is impossible. And I love our relationship like it is. I'd be an idiot to fuck this up. God knows that I'm not any good at romantic relationships. My track record is bleak and I don't feel like I have that much to offer. But before these thoughts can get away with me—though they've done their best to make me feel like shit—we pull into the church parking lot and Cash finds a spot, then kills the engine.

"Well, here we are," he says. I force a smile and his gaze lingers on me. "What's wrong?" he asks.

"Nothing," I lie. I do my best to give my smile an authentic varnish, but he sees through it. He does me a favor though and doesn't bring it up again, letting me stew on my own in weird thoughts. But I realize quickly that now is not the time to be weighing the consequences of a romantic relationship. Now is the time to be thinking about what we can find out from Holly.

I get out of the truck. Surely Holly has some insight into their relationship, having taught at the same school.

We walk over to the entrance and people are coming and going. Holloway is nowhere to be found, but his name is on everyone's lips. I hope that what happened is enough to disgrace him, but I don't think Holloway is the kind of person who has the good sense or decency to feel anything akin to shame. Hopefully, I'm wrong. But just in case I'm not, I keep an eye out for him. The last thing I want is another confrontation with him today while I'm trying to glean whatever info I can from Holly. And it's then that we spot her in the atrium, talking to a kid who I imagine is a student of hers. She pats him on the shoulder and he goes on his way. And we seize our chance.

"Holly!" I say over the conversation going on in the atrium. People more about, back and forth, finding their way in and out to whatever talk they're planning to attend next. Holly stands there, looks around, and finally lands her eyes on us and her face lights up.

"Hey, guys!" she says, patting me on the arm when I walk up. "Good to see the two of you. Where's Lisa and Clayton?"

"They stayed home today," Cash says with a smile.

"Holly," I say. "I wanted to ask you some questions," I lower my voice.

"Let's go over here," Cash says, leading us off the side where we won't be in the way of people walking. Holly follows obediently, and her eyebrow arches in interest when I turn to face her.

"What's up?" she asks.

"I wanted to see what you know about Haley Stone," I say. "And her relationship with Michael Berkley."

"Oh," she says. "She was his star pupil. His favorite far and above everyone else. He was always bragging about how good she was at cross-country. Saying that there was no doubt in his mind she would get a scholarship. Hard worker and smart, too. She aced all of her classes. Straight-A student for her entire life," Holly says.

"Do you think that Michael might have told her where he was going before he disappeared?" Cash asks.

"Gosh," Holly says. "I don't know. They were close, though. He was a mentor to her. He was always giving her advice and making sure she was okay. Her home life is a little rough," she adds.

"Rough how?" I ask.

"Her mom rules that house with an iron fist," Holly says. "It's no secret that she gives all of Haley's teachers fits. I'm sure it was the same with Michael. The Stone family is extremely religious. And religious people rarely like education that strays from the path, if you know what I mean. I'm sure she was concerned that Michael was filling Haley's head with all kinds of ideas about leaving Hobby Hollow and going somewhere else. Somewhere worldly."

"So you think Linda had a problem with Michael?" I ask.

"Not to the point of making him disappear, if that's what you're asking. She actually said nothing to me about it. I was one of the few teachers she had the patience for. Thought I was a good Christian girl," she adds with a laugh.

"Well, thank you," I say. "I just wondered if Haley might know what happened to him."

"I really don't think so," Holly says. "I think if she did, she adored that teacher so much that she would have been the first in line to tell about it." Cash nods, and I glance back at Holly. Just then, she excuses herself. "Sorry, I really want to hear this guy speak," she says. And then she tells us goodbye.

Right around the time that I'm turning to talk to Cash, I see Linda and Haley Stone walk in to the same presentation. Haley wears bright pink Adidas running shoes that look faded from the sun. Track pants cover her long legs, and she wears her hair in a bun with a large Hobby Hollow high sweatshirt. Part of me wants to go over to Haley and demand that she tell me what she knows about when Michael Berkley went missing.

CHAPTER THIRTY-THREE

CASH'S PHONE RINGS, and he reaches for his back pocket. My attention shifts away from Haley and Linda and back to my companion. He swipes to answer and immediately gets a look of concern on his face.

"We'll be right there," he says into the receiver, and then looks at me.

"What?" I ask.

"The police are headed over to Clayton's. Say they've got some more questions for us about the lanyard and the planner," he says, now looking concerned himself. I arch an eyebrow, wondering what they could want to talk about now, and the two of us head for the truck. I buckle my seatbelt and turn my attention to Cash.

"What do you think they want?" I ask.

"There's no telling," Cash says. "I wonder if they found out anything from the planner." I nod. That could be it. That was quick. Maybe they could x-ray the thing and find out more that way, without having to wait for it to dry out. I rack my brain, thinking of all the true crime shows I've watched, wondering if there's an answer in some of that knowledge. But I come up empty-handed and we head back to the house. When we pull up, there's a police cruiser already waiting there. And the cops are nowhere to be found.

"They must be inside," Cash says. The two of us hurry for the front door and throw it open, seeing the two cops sitting in the living room with Clayton and Lisa sitting in front of them.

"Sorry it took us so long," Cash offers.

"No problem," one of them says, standing to shake our hands. "We just wanted to ask you guys a few more questions about the lanyard and the planner."

"No problem at all," Cash echoes what the cop just said. I nod, and the two of us take the chairs opposite each other on either far side of the living room.

"So," the other officer says. I look at him with rapt attention, feeling instantly nervous even though we've done nothing wrong. Something about cops makes everyone nervous, I think. Just seeing them makes you feel guilty about everything bad you've ever done in your life, even if it wasn't illegal. "We just wanted to hear a bit more about this location where the stuff was found," the officer says. He looks at me.

"Well," I say. "We went hiking up there the first day we came down."

"I showed her the place," Cash interjects. "Clayton and I used to hike and camp there. It's tucked out of the way."

"Can you show us on a map?" The other officer asks, laying out a small map of the area. Cash grabs the pen that he hands him and marks the area.

"Right there," Cash says.

"That is out of the way," the cop remarks. "How'd you know about it?" he presses.

"We used to go there," he eyes Clayton somewhat nervously. I look over at Clayton and he looks like he's going to be sick. I mentally urge him to get his shit together. The cop looks him over.

"Why did you guys go up there?" the cop asks Clayton.

"It probably sounds ridiculous," Clayton says with a laugh, regaining his composure. "But we went up there to look for Bigfoot," he tells the officer. The officer raises an eyebrow and looks at his companion, who smirks.

"Not too ridiculous down here," the other officer says. "I got an uncle that swears he's seen the thing." I smile and Cash offers a laugh. The tension seems to break somewhat.

"What would Michael have been doing up there?" One cop asks Clayton. His gaze is piercing.

"Oh," Clayton says. "Well, I took him up there a while back. When he was having trouble with that girl-friend of his, who moved away. Thought it might be a nice place for him to think." I almost reach for my phone, wanting to show them the picture where Michael had someone take a shot of him looking out over the ridge. As if that will absolve Clayton of any guilt and make them look elsewhere. I'm not sure that it would, though, so I say nothing.

"Okay," the officer says, making some notes on his pad. Then he folds it closed and tucks it into his pocket, standing.

"I think that's all we needed," the other officer says. "Just wanted to know why Michael would have been up there. Sounds like he was going through a hell of a time with his girlfriend," he remarks.

"It certainly seemed that way to me," Clayton says. The two officers shake all of our hands and head for the door.

"Thanks for getting us that planner," one of them says as they exit through the door. I furrow my brow, wondering about that. We wave goodbye as they pull out in their cruiser and the four of us head back inside.

Clayton breathes a deep sigh of relief, and Lisa rubs his back, apparently over her anger at the money he gave to Michael. I look at Cash, the statement the cop made about the planner still staying with me. Haley's planner. What would be in there? Instantly, I wonder if she made a note or something about what Michael told her when they were up there. Maybe where he was going. I make a mental note to follow up on that with Cash when we get a minute.

Clayton and Lisa head into the kitchen and Clayton tells us he's going to order lunch and work on some stuff in his office. Lisa says she's going to lie down for a nap. We give Clayton our orders and the two of us sit down at the kitchen table by ourselves. I seize the opportunity to ask Cash about the planner and my suspicions.

"Do you think Haley made a note of where he was going?" I ask.

"Or maybe how to contact him," Cash offers. I hadn't thought of that, but it makes perfect sense.

"Do you think she's in contact with him?" I ask. "And why would he disappear without a trace? Along with Clayton's money?"

"I'm not sure," Cash says. "It's like he was running from something. Like he lied about the money. The reason he needed it. He said something to Clayton that he knew would get to him. That he knew would resonate with him. The fertility treatments."

"But he and his girlfriend split right before he disappeared," I say. Cash nods at this. "What would he have needed the money for otherwise?" I ask.

"I'm not sure," Cash says. "But I'm guessing he needed to pay someone off. He had a debt or something. Or he'd gotten involved with dirty business trying to earn the money he needed for the treatments. Maybe it was the breaking point for her," he offers.

It makes sense. Maybe she just got sick of him

trying to get the money in ways that were less than legal. And then she split, leaving him in the dust.

"Maybe it was," I say. I know that I'd be fed up if my boyfriend kept getting involved with heroin rings and the like. Maybe she'd just had enough.

"I can imagine a woman saying that she wouldn't want to raise a child with someone who will do that to get the money they need. She might have felt like she couldn't trust him," Cash says. I roll this over in my mind, knowing that there's really only one way to find out.

"We have to find her," I tell Cash. "We need to talk to her and find out from her why she left Michael."

CHAPTER THIRTY-FOUR

CASH and I head up to my room and I get my laptop out, plopping onto the bed in front of it. He sits at the end, waiting patiently. I navigate to the notes that I made when I looked at her info for the first time. When I got an e-mail address and phone number for her. I get out my phone and dial the number. Then I hit the button to call her.

"Here we go," I tell Cash. He crosses fingers on both of his hands and holds them up, biting his bottom lip in a hopeful expression. I nod, putting the phone on speaker. But after just two rings, the call goes straight to voicemail and I hang up, defeated. I sigh.

"Is there another number for her?" he asks. "Like a place of employment or something?"

I go back to her Facebook profile and find the non-profit that she's currently working. Then I jot that down on a note and Google the number for it. After a few keystrokes and pushing a few buttons on the screen of my phone, we're connected to the reception-ist. My eyes widen when she picks up. I guess I wasn't really expecting the call to go through, but it does.

"Hello, Rivergate Foundation, this is Sherry. How can I help you?" a peppy female voice says on the other end of the call.

"Yes, umm," I hesitate, getting my bearings. "Is there any way I could speak to Melanie Carter?" I look at Cash for guidance and he nods his head, giving me a thumb up gesture.

"Well, she's currently in a meeting, but I could take a message for you and have her call you back," Sherry says pleasantly.

"Umm, yeah," I say. "That would be perfect." Cash nods, encouraging me. "Here's my number and my name is Blair. Tell her I was just wanting to touch base with her on something." Sherry makes an affirmative noise and I can hear her scratching down my info and my message with a pen and paper.

"Will do, Blair!" Sherry says happily. And then she hangs up. I lay the phone on the bed and look up at Cash.

"Well," I say. "I guess that's that. And now we wait."

To pass the time until we get a call back from Melanie, Cash and I go back to the festival. I scan the crowd when we walk inside, looking for Holloway, and I spot him, holding court over a group of people in the atrium, a coffee in the hand he gestures widely with, surely telling them what an unfair shake he's gotten with everything.

"Look who it is," Cash says under his breath. "The snake oil salesman himself."

I have no desire to have an interaction with Holloway, but I notice that he's got Karen Dunham at his mercy, parading out her story for the people in front of him and something tugs at my basic sense of right and wrong. Before I can help myself, I'm headed over there. Holloway spots me as I come walking up.

"Well, what have we here?" he says, looking over at me as I approach. I motion at Karen.

"Do you have a minute, Karen?" I ask. Her eyes find mine and for a moment, I swear I read relief there. She's as eager to get away from Holloway as I am. It only serves to confirm my idea that she's being taken advantage of, and she's seeing that. Likely, the only reason she went with Holloway's way of doing things was because the police didn't listen to her. All Holloway cared about was being able to exploit Karen, however he could to get his name back on the bill. And he'd managed that, I guess. He got to present his wild ass theories about Michael Berkley's disappearance. And he got to lead an expedition once again. Although he ended up shooting an innocent person in the course of all of that.

"Don't you have some police questioning to follow

up on?" I ask him sourly. His eyes flash with anger. Clearly I've hit a nerve.

"I wouldn't know anything about that, seeing as how I did nothing wrong," Holloway says. I glare at him and then turn my gaze to Karen, willing her to come with me. She takes a step forward, but Holloway stops her. "You don't want to go talk to this nasty lady, Karen," he says to her.

Cash steps up behind me.

"If he's making you stand here against your will, I'll stop it," Cash says to Karen. She looks at him pleadingly.

"Leave her alone, Holloway," I say. Karen squeezes out of the group of people and they turn their angry eyes on me, Cash, and Karen. We squirrel Karen out of the building and she thanks us. Her speech slurs, and obviously she's started drinking already for the day. The sight makes my heart hurt. I think of my brother, wondering if he's become an alcoholic these days. Back when we were younger, he drank a lot.

Karen thanks us, and she heads for her vehicle. I almost stop her, but she's too quick and doesn't want any help.

"What an asshole," I say, referencing Holloway.

"You got that right," Cash says. And then I feel my phone vibrate in my pocket. I pull it out and look at the caller ID. It says "unknown."

"Answer it!" Cash urges me. It doesn't instantly register with me it could be Melanie. But it makes sense. I imagine she doesn't want us knowing her real number. I pick it up and put it on speakerphone as Cash and I step outside and head for the truck.

"Hello?" I say, just as we both shut our doors.

"Yeah, who is this and what do you want?" Melanie asks. Her tone makes no room for small talk. She's all business, and I assume she already knows that we want to talk about Michael.

"My name is Blair and–" I say, but she cuts me off. I look up at Cash as she speaks.

"If this is about Michael, I don't have any idea where he is," she says. "I just know that he probably pissed off the wrong people."

My eyes widen, and I try to think of what to say.

"Who did he piss off?" I ask.

"I can't tell you that," Melanie says.

"When was the last time you saw him?" Cash asks, interjecting himself into the conversation. Melanie hesitates for a moment, and I think she's not going to answer. But then she speaks.

"All I know is that the last time he saw me, he gave me 10,000 dollars and told me to keep my mouth shut about anything I knew. But I knew nothing," she says, and her tone seems to soften. "I just figured he was into something bad if he was giving me ten grand."

"What would he have wanted you to keep your mouth shut about?" I ask.

"I don't even know. He was acting different

towards the end," Melanie says. "Secretive. Like he was cheating on me."

"Do you think he was?" I ask. "I thought you guys were going through fertility treatments." She laughs bitterly.

"Hell no, we weren't," she says. "Is that what someone told you?" she asks. "That's a laugh. Michael and I were on the rocks almost all the time. We were never serious enough about each other to try for a baby."

"Do you know if Michael might have told someone that you were seeking those treatments?" I ask her, probing for the reason Michael might have given her the money. She's evasive then.

"Why don't you ask his other girlfriend?" she asks. "I think he paid me off to get me to forget about how awful he was to me. Michael had this good guy appearance on the outside, but inside he was a monster. He was awful to me. And I think he found somebody new and just wanted me to fuck right on off so he could ride off into the sunset." I start to pose another question, but Melanie cuts me off.

"So go ask her. I have nothing else to say," she says. And she hangs up the phone.

CHAPTER THIRTY-FIVE

"WE NEED to go back to the festival," I tell Cash, my tone urgent. I stand up from the bed and snap my laptop shut.

"What are we going to do?" he asks.

"I'm going to talk to Haley," I tell him. "I think maybe it should just be me. She might be more comfortable talking to a woman than to..." I look at him. "A large man," I say.

"I'm trying to take that as a compliment," Cash says.

"It's for the best that you do," I tease him, and head out of the bedroom and down the stairs. I grab my jacket once again from the coat rack and Cash does the same.

"See you guys after awhile," he hollers back at Clayton and Lisa as we leave the house and head for his truck. Cash makes quick work of the drive from

Clayton and Lisa's over to the church where the festival is.

The place is packed, though not as packed as it was yesterday. I wonder if there are people who were driven off by Holloway's ridiculous show of idiocy. That's my assumption as we walk in. Just as we enter, one of the talks is about to begin and I spot Linda and Haley with Nathan—the guy whose property we investigated the other night.

They're laughing and talking, but the smiles don't quite reach Haley's eyes. Cash and I walk over to her and her mom and cousin. Nathan spots us first and clears his throat, no longer laughing.

"Hey there," he says to the two of us. I glance back at Cash, urging him to talk to Nathan and I hope he can read the expression on my face. Thankfully he does, and he starts talking to the man. "This is my aunt and her daughter, my cousin Haley," Nathan says, by way of introduction. "These are some of the people that came out to investigate my place the other night," he tells Linda.

Linda gives me a sour look, like she can't imagine what I would be annoying her with my presence for. And I don't really have any good excuse. The only thing I can think to tell her is the truth, which is that I want to question her daughter about whether she knows where Michael is. But I resist the urge to say that. Instead, I try something else.

"Holly told me all about you," I tell Haley. "Said

that you're going to get a scholarship from running," I mention. Linda bristles at that.

"We'll see," she says.

"Probably not now," Haley says, rolling her eyes at her mom and giving me a languishing look that teens seem to have perfected.

"We better head in there if we're going to catch what this lady has to say," Nathan says to the two of them. Linda lets him take her arm in his and they start that way. But Haley hangs back. Just the opportunity I was looking for.

"Why not now?" I ask her, already knowing the answer.

"Coach Berkley is gone," she says, and her voice cracks at the end of the sentence.

"I heard you were his favorite on the team," I tell her, trying to give her some sense of consolation, but she doesn't seem to take it.

"They just want me to stay here forever," she says, glancing over her shoulder, seemingly to see if her mom and Nathan are hanging around where they can hear her, but they aren't. Haley looks back at me.

"Did you know him or something?" she asks me. There's trepidation in her tone. Like she thinks I'm going to tell her I know she knows where he is. But I don't. Cash hangs back, unoccupied but doing his best not to be obtrusive. I glance over at him, leaning against the wall, checking his phone and furtively glancing up at us from time to time.

"I didn't," I tell her honestly. "I only recently heard about him going missing. My friend and I are just here for this festival," I tell her, gesturing around us. I look down at Haley's feet and see those pink, sun-faded Adidas again. And I try to remember why they're familiar. But nothing comes to mind. It niggles in the back of my brain, though, urging me to figure out the answer. Urging me to figure out why I know those shoes and why it bothers me so much.

"Listen, Haley," I say. "You're a smart girl. And I know that Mr. Berkley really saw something in you," I add. She looks up at me, her eyes almost pleading. Like she needed to hear that. "And I'm sure you'll get out of this town if you want to," I reassure her. "But I need to ask you some questions about Mr. Berkley and where he went."

Haley seems to get nervous, almost like she's not sure if she wants to continue our conversation. I glance up to make sure that her mom isn't hovering in the doorway or hasn't sent Nathan to see what I'm up to with her daughter. But good fortune has it that neither of them are making an appearance.

"Did he tell you he was leaving?" I ask her.

"No," she says, her voice ont he verge of tears. I want to tell her it's okay. That everything's going to be fine. But the teacher that had told her she had a shot out of this place is gone, and likely dead. All I want to do is figure out why he went missing in the first place.

"Are you sure?" I ask her.

"We know he had your planner before he went missing. Were you hanging out with him?" I look at her, wondering how that will hit her. And boy, do I get a reaction out of the girl. Her eyes go wide, her lip trembles.

"No!" Haley says. "I don't know why he had it. I must have left it in his classroom. And he didn't tell me anything because there was nothing for him to tell," she says. "Someone made him leave," she adds. "They made him disappear." She spits out the final words as if she's spraying venom in my direction. I back up at her outburst.

"Haley," I say. "If you know anything, you have to tell the police," I tell her.

"I don't know anything!" she almost shouts. People standing around us in the atrium look up. Cash does, too, and shifts his weight, almost like he's planning on walking over to us to break it up. Haley turns on her heel and heads for the room where the presentation is taking place. I turn and see Cash walking over to where we just stood talking.

"Well, that went well," he says. "I don't suppose she'll be up for another round of questioning by you later. Good thing I didn't come over here and mess it up," he adds. But he has a smirk on his face.

"Yeah, I guess I pushed her too hard," I say, suddenly feeling guilty. I had wanted to come across as someone she could trust, but wanting the answers so bad made me too aggressive with her.

"It's okay," he says. "I heard most of it. So at least you don't need to catch me up on where we are in this thing," he says, trying to sound positive. I smile at him.

"At least there's that," I say.

"So Haley doesn't know anything more about why Michael disappeared than Melanie does," Cash concludes. And I'm thinking much the same thing. "All we know is that he wasn't taken away in a spaceship by Bigfoot and that he disappeared with three people. If Bigfoot who took him is a person, and I'm assuming he is." I halfway listen to Cash's assessment as I get out my phone to look through Michael's pictures again. The ones that I saved from his social media profiles. I scroll through them once, then twice. Then I look back at Cash.

"So now what do we do?" I ask.

"I guess we can go back to the drawing board," he suggests. "If Michael didn't tell anyone that he was going to disappear, then either he didn't know he was going to disappear or he was making a hell of an effort to completely vanish from the grid." Cash rubs his jaw as he thinks this over.

"Wait," I say, something dawning on me. Cash starts to say something and I silence him, holding a hand up, indicating he has to be quiet for me to think. "Wait," I repeat. And I grab my phone once more and start scrolling through the pictures again. And then I see it.

I stare at it for a moment and enlarge the picture,

wondering if my eyes are playing tricks on me. Finally, I show the image to Cash.

"What am I looking at?" he asks, not seeing it at first.

"What do you see in that picture?" I ask him.

"I see Michael Berkley, posing on that ridge," he says, his face puzzled.

"Look in the corner," I say. Cash does and his eyes widen.

"Are those..."

"Pink Adidas," I say. "Just like the one's on Haley's feet today."

"That means that she was there with Michael right before he disappeared," Cash says.

"I think I know who the other girl was in his life," I say.

CHAPTER THIRTY-SIX

CASH STARES at the screen and then looks at me. He glances up in the direction that Haley went.

"You don't think...?" he begins to say but stops midway through the question.

"I do," I say. "Oh my God, it all makes sense." I run a hand through my hair. Someone on the other side of the room sees me making a scene and stares.

"Let's go outside," I tell Cash. Quickly the two of us step out of the atrium into the covered walkway between parts of the building.

"It makes sense," I tell Cash before we stop walking. I whisper in case anyone is out here, potentially listening.

"I think you might be on to something," Cash says.

"I think she was more than just his student and his athlete," I tell Cash. "She was the one who took the picture of him at the ridge. I think she was there more than once, more than twice. She's the reason he wanted his girlfriend out of the picture."

"So, he paid Melanie off to get her to leave?" Cash asks.

"Or Melanie threatened to go to the cops and he paid her off, then she left of her own volition," I suggest.

"Who was in the truck?" Cash asks. '

"Someone big," I say. Just as I say that to Cash, Nathan comes walking out of the room where the presentation is taking place. I spot him instantly.

"Hey," I say.

"Howdy," Nathan says, apparently none the wiser to what my conversation with Haley was about while he was in that room.

"Nathan, what do you know about Michael Berkley going missing?" Cash asks, cutting right to the chase. Nathan is caught off guard by the question and hems and haws around an answer. He searches for one, obviously bewildered by the rapid fire question Cash threw at him.

"Well, I think maybe he was doing things he shouldn't have been," he says, pointing obliquely at the truth.

"Like sleeping with a student?" I ask. Nathan eyes me. All of his charming, good old boy demeanor evaporates. He gives me a piercing stare, like he wants to rip my head off.

"You shouldn't' go messing in things you don't understand," Nathan says, a threat in his tone. He moves toward me and Cash steps up.

"You sure you don't know anything about that, Nathan?" Cash asks. I stare at their towering figures and thinking about what Nathan might look like out in the moonlight. If he could be mistaken for a Bigfoot by a drunk. I think the answer to that is obvious. He absolutely could be mistaken for something else. Something much larger. Something much less human. And he could have dragged Michael off into the woods.

Just as I'm about to question him some more, the door bursts open and Linda and Haley come out.

"Now what are you bothering him for?" Linda shouts at Cash. People are streaming out of the building, coming from this presentation or that. A crowd starts to gather, sensing the beginnings of a dramatic scene. I hear murmurs in the crowd and glance around. People are whispering back and forth, eager for some kind of confrontation. Linda steps up beside Nathan and Haley hangs back, tears in her eyes.

"I'll ask you again," Linda says. "What are you harassing my nephew for?" she asks.

"Just trying to figure out why Michael Berkley went missing," Cash says. "And why your daughter's planner was found in a location that only Michael knew about, along with Michael's lanyard."

Linda's face turns beet red and Haley cries into her hands behind them. Holly steps out of the church building, looking to see what all the commotion is about.

"He absolutely got what was coming to him," Linda says, her tone furious. Her eyes blaze with anger and I'm sure that if she could burn a hole in Cash right now, she would. It's right about then that the crowd parts, making way for two officers. The same two officers that came by Clayton's house earlier.

One of them makes eye contact with me and looks a little surprised to see Cash and I right in the middle of things. I want to tell him he should never be surprised to find Cash in the middle of anything, and I guess me either for that matter. I seem to have done a good job of inserting myself down here where I didn't belong.

"Linda and Nathan Stone?" the cop asks Linda and Nathan. The two of them look away from me and Cash, their eyes finding the officers.

"It's not their fault!" Haley shouts, tears in her eyes. The seventeen year old girl throws herself down in a heap in front of the police officers, like a scene out of a movie. "This is all my fault," she shouts. She begins to sob loudly. The crowd quiets as she starts to speak. "They only did this because they thought they were saving me from myself," Haley cries out. "But I loved him and he loved me. I know he was my teacher, but it didn't matter. We knew the whole lot of you would never understand," she points at the crowd.

"And they thought they were protecting me," she points at Linda and Nathan.

Her confession washes over all of us. The crowd and me and Cash. The officers, too.

"We saw your notes in the planner, Haley," one of the officers said. "And the last note you made in it, about Nathan and Linda making Michael go away," the other one finishes.

I look at Linda and she clutches her throat. Almost like a lady might clutch her pearls. I can tell she's nervous. That she's been caught.

"You two are under arrest," one of the officers says, and they move to put cuffs on both of them. Haley remains on the ground and Holly swoops over to help her up. Sniffling, Haley collapses into Holly's arms and she holds the girl tight. I feel for her. I really do. She's too young to know that she was preyed on. That Michael Berkley wasn't out for anyone but himself.

I instantly wonder if we did the right thing. If maybe we shouldn't have just let the whole thing be.

Maybe Michael deserved to disappear. Maybe Haley would be better off coping in private and reckoning with all of this on her own, in her own time.

Maybe we fucked up.

I swallow hard, watching the scene play out in front of us. They arrest Linda and Nathan and they go wordlessly. Haley stays behind with Holly and the cops take her statement, too. They explain all of the evidence that they found and my head is swimming with all of it.

Apparently Haley used her planner as a diary as much as an agenda. And she'd made notes about Michael's actions in it. She also seemed to have made ample notes about what actually happened to Michael after Nathan and Linda got a hold of him. Haley helps them as much as she can and they thank her for her statement and cooperation. Then they get the crowd to dissipate.

I think about going over to her. Going to say something, but I can't find the right words. In my heart of hearts I know the right word is sorry. I shouldn't have pushed it, and by the time that we get into Cash's truck, I feel like I'm going to throw up.

"Are you okay?" Cash asks as he buckles his seatbelt and I do the same. I catch sight of myself in the sideview mirror and see that I'm looking almost green.

"I don't know," I tell him honestly. "I feel like maybe we didn't do the right thing."

Cash is quiet for a moment, and his silence makes me wonder if he's thinking the same thing. That maybe we should have just let it be.

"We did the right thing, Blair," Cash tells me. And we head back over to Clayton and Lisa's. I roll this over in my mind all the way there, wondering if Cash is right. I'm not so sure. At least not as sure as he seems to be. That's for certain.

Shortly thereafter, we pull up into the driveway of

the house we've called home for the last few days. I sit in the truck for a moment after Cash gets out and I look up at Clayton and Lisa's beautiful home. I think about Haley Stone and I wonder if I did right by her. And I'm certain that until I know, it will weigh on me as heavy as her last name.

CHAPTER THIRTY-SEVEN

BY THE TIME we get into the house, the sun is setting and Clayton and Lisa are talking about dinner.

"Well, you missed it," Cash says to Clayton as he takes off his jacket and hangs it on the coat rack. I do the same but far more quietly, still feeling a little sick after my self-reflection on the way over here.

"No, I'm afraid I didn't," Clayton says. "It was all over Facebook before the two of you got back. Linda and Nathan got arrested."

I sit down oat the dining table and Cash goes and grabs us two beers. He sits one in front of me and grabs the chair across the table from me. Clayton orders a pizza and grabs himself a beer and a water for Lisa, and they come sit down to join us.

"So what happened?" Lisa asks.

"I told her about the planner and the lanyard," Clayton interjects, probably trying to make the telling of the tale a little easier. Cash looks at me, deferring to my explanation. I nod, and begin.

"When we found the planner, we couldn't get it open. And it was laying there on top of the ridge with the lanyard, which made both of us think that it had belonged to MIchael, too." I glance over at Cash and get his confirmation. "Anyway, we talked to Karen Dunham after Holloway put on that ridiculous performance out at the farm. And she told us that she actually saw Bigfoot get into a pick up truck with two other people. But at that point, we weren't sure who it was. We were still thinking that it might have been someone that Michael was mixed up with business-wise." I look at Cash, gesturing to him to let him know that he can tell the rest.

"Anyway, we figured out that Haley had been up there with Michael more than just once. We'd thought it had to do with his disappearance. That maybe he'd told her where he was going. But it turned out Michael was involved with Haley, probably manipulating her and likely thinking he could get away with it without anyone finding out that he'd been preying on his students. I wouldn't be surprised if more girls come forward after this gets around town."

"Wow," Clayton says.

"So Haley's mom and Nathan were the ones that took care of Michael. I guess that maybe he was planning on meeting Haley out at the farm that night and Nathan ambushed him. I can see why Karen would think he was a Sasquatch. The dude's huge," Cash goes on. "Haley saw the whole thing. She was the one who confessed for the both of them. Told the cops his body was below that ridge where we found the lanyard and the planner. I hope she'll be alright."

"Holly already called me and said she's taking care of Haley for the time being. She'll be in good hands," Lisa says. The four of us hash and rehash it for some time, sitting in the living room. Finally, it's mid-afternoon and sunset is fast approaching. Lisa and Clayton fix dinner and Cash and I step outside onto the little screened in patio with the heater. He's been put in charge of watching the baked potatoes on the grill. After checking them, he comes and sits down beside me.

"Heck of a weekend," Cash says. I nod, nursing the beer that he brought me. He sips on one of his own.

"That's one way of putting it," I remark with a chuckle.

"Do you rate it higher or lower than ghost hunting?" Cash asks with a smile.

"Oh, that's a tough one," I say. A grin at him and feel my heart beating faster in my chest. I feel a flush of heat on my cheeks.

"I think it's a tie," Cash says.

"Oh, why's that?" I ask, arching an eyebrow. The flames from the fire keep the little enclosed space warm and Cash is sitting so close to me that I can feel the heat from his body, too. I want to reach for his hand.

But I don't. He looks up at me over his beer, our knees touching. He places a hand on my knee then, and his eyes meet mine. His lips part. Mine do too. My eyes dart to his mouth. And he leans in.

"I got to be with you, either way," he says, his voice husky. My heart is in my throat. Then the door opens. Cash pulls back and the moment is gone.

"Those about ready?" Clayton asks about the potatoes.

"I'll check," Cash says and he hops up. I almost want to yell at Clayton for interrupting the moment. But as the romantic haze begins to clear, circulating away in the cool air, I wonder again if it's even that good of an idea. That we might not be better off as friends. But then I think about all these little moments. I watch Cash at the grill and I stare at him. I watch him check the potatoes and pull them off, only a plate.

Clayton comes out and helps him carry everything in and shut down the grill. I grab both of our beers and we all head inside. The evening is pleasant. The conversation warm. And the company is the best.

I catch Cash looking at me over dinner a few times. And once again I catch Clayton giving one or both of us a smirk. Finally, everyone's ready for bed. Finally, both of us head up to our rooms.

I step inside of mine and turn, watching Cash shut the door to his room. All that remains is the final day of the festival and I lean against the door, then slide down it quietly, sitting in the floor like I'm a teenager. I keep thinking about that moment. That almost kiss. And I wonder if he's in the other room thinking about the same thing.

Finally I get up off the floor and head over to the bed. I slip out of my jeans and shirt and into some pajamas and then crawl into bed. I close my eyes and find that up until the moment I fall asleep, I'm thinking of Cash.

CHAPTER THIRTY-EIGHT

THE LAST DAY of the festival arrives. There's little on the schedule but this evening, they're going to have people telling stories around the campfire again. And I'm looking forward to it. As I get ready, I think about how I entered this entire experience: completely skeptical. And then I think about the experiences that I was blessed to have down here. Not just helping solve the mystery of what happened to Michael, but even more so the experience that I got to have in the woods with Katie Reinhart and Cash. I'll never forget that.

I head downstairs and see everyone already gathered at the kitchen table, Clayton once again making breakfast. It makes me smirk. I hope Lisa keeps making him make breakfast, digging his way out of the doghouse. It won't hurt him. And besides, she's almost nine months pregnant.

I catch Cash's eye as I hit the bottom of the stairs

and he looks at me, his eyes lingering on me for longer than absolutely necessary. I try to read something there, but he's looking back at Clayton just then. And maybe I'm reading too much into things. Maybe I should just let it go.

We all have a bite to eat and then Clayton and Lisa clear the table. I help them and Cash sips his coffee. After the dishes are loaded, I head back over to the table and join him with a cup of my own. I drank orange juice with breakfast.

"So, what's the plan for today?" I ask.

"Well, there are a few talks at the festival we could go see. The main attraction tonight is the campfire stories again, though," he says.

"I want to be there for that. Then we can head out. Make it home around midnight. How does that sound?" he asks.

"It sounds good to me," I say.

"I can't believe you guys are leaving already," Lisa says. "I've loved having you here," she tells us.

"Same, buddy," Clayton says. "It's been too long since I last saw you. We gotta fix that." Cash nods.

"Way too long," he says. "I'll be back more often, I promise."

I hope Cash is going to keep that promise. I know how easy it is to tell someone that you'll keep in touch and then not be able to follow through. Sometimes life just gets in the way and before we know it, it's later than we think.

I think about my dad. I always thought we'd have time to fix whatever had gone wrong between us. But it turns out we didn't after all. I want to tell him that. Tell him I thought we'd have time. But I know there's no way to do that. Not now. He really is gone, most likely. And if he isn't, how could I forgive him if I found out he's been alive the whole time and just hadn't told me? It's a deeper thought than I want to entertain at breakfast, so I push it away, forcing a smile onto my face as everyone talks about what they'll do the next time they see each other. And part of me hopes I'll be included in that.

Cash and I go over to the festival to catch the last of the speakers that afternoon. It's a little slower going, with talks that aren't as exciting scheduled for the last day. I imagine many people head out before Sunday night, and by the time the sun is about to set, the place looks like a ghost town compared to how it looked when we first arrived.

I still see Katie's vehicles and a few others that I recognize from traipsing through the lot repeatedly. But I don't see Holloway, and I'm relieved. It's after the last talk that Katie catches up with us to give us an update about him.

"I guess you guys already heard the news, huh?" she asks Cash and me. I glance up at Cash, wondering if he knows something that I don't. But he looks back at me, puzzled. A wide grin spreads on Katie's face. She's obviously eager to replay some information.

"What?" I ask, unable to wait any longer.

"Holloway got charged for shooting that guy," she says. "His ass is currently sitting in jail."

I laugh, a smile breaking out across my face.

"It's where he belongs," Cash says. His tone is more serious. "I wish there was a way to get him for exploiting Karen, but this will do. Maybe keep him out of trouble for a while," he adds.

"We can all hope," Katie says. "Are you guys sticking around for the fire tonight?" she asks.

"We are," I say. Looking at Cash for confirmation, he nods.

"Good," she says. "I think it'll be fun." Katie turns to go but I stop her, walking up to her as she's leaving.

"Katie," I say. And she turns. "I just want to thank you for letting us going out into the woods with you. I've never—" I try to find the words.

"Changed your entire perspective, didn't it?" she asks, cutting me off. A wide grin is on her face.

"You could say that," I tell her with a smile. She nods and squeezes my hand and leaves us. I turn back to Cash and walk over to him, my arms folded across my chest.

"Hell of a weekend," I say, repeating his words from earlier in the week. And he just smiles, understanding exactly what I mean.

Finally, the sun sets and with the darkness comes an influx of people to the amphitheater in the campgrounds. Cash and I snag seats that are closer to the stage this time and there are quite a few less people here this time around, too. I gather that my suspicion was wright. Lots of people have already headed home from the festival. We're the diehards tonight. Us and about fifty to one hundred other people.

They gather slowly, filling up part of the amphitheater, with more space between each other this time. And unfortunately, that means that there's more space between Cash and me, too. A few people tell their stories. Several of them describe the sounds that you hear in the woods when you're looking for Bigfoot. That howl that's almost a scream and the way it sends a chill down your spine or brings tears to your eyes just because your body recognizes it as so foreign and so unnatural. Like nothing you've ever heard.

It makes me think about our experience in the woods and how it felt to hear that first hand. I glance over at Cash a few times, wondering how he's feeling hearing these stories, and he returns me a warm smile twice.

I'm suddenly glad that I went down here this weekend. It occurs to me just how lonely I was before I met Cash. I spent most of my evenings in front of the television. I hadn't had an adventure in years.

And then I think about my dad. Is this what it was like for him? Constant adventures? I can see the appeal of that now.

After the last speaker sits down, Charlie hands off

the microphone for Katie to close the festival. She steps up, illuminated by firelight, and speaks.

"I'm so glad that you all could join us for another successful festival, minus some unfortunate events," she says, and a few people in the crowd–likely not fans of Holloway's–chuckle. She goes on. "This is an ever evolving realm of information. And I know that we're looked down on by the other parts of the scientific community, considered pseudoscience by them. But I want to remind you all not to discount your experiences. Make notes of them, record them, keep them. There is something going on out there, and I think many of us have experienced it firsthand." She looks directly at me and smiles. I smile back at her. "Now, have a safe trip home and we hope to see you next year," she concludes, handing the microphone back to Charlie as everyone applauds. Charlie says a few words and dismisses the crowd. Cash stands and looks at me.

"Are you ready?" he asks.

"As I'm going to be," I say, sort of reluctant to leave the whole thing behind. But I follow him to his truck, where our bags are already loaded up, packed up back at Clayton and Lisa's before we came out here. Our goodbyes have been said, and somehow I feel weird leaving.

Cash unlocks the truck and both of us get inside. He starts the engine and we head for the main road,

...as back to the highway and all the way

...ness, I speak. Only the glow of the dash

...er of us.

...hink we did the right thing?" I ask him. Cash is quiet for a moment.

"What do you think, Blair?" he asks. "What would your dad have done?"

"I don't know," I say, somewhat defensively. Once again reminded of how little I knew of him.

"Well, I can tell you," Cash says. "He would have chased the truth down no matter where it was going to lead him. And you did just that." He looks over at me in the darkness. I think that over for a second. It is what I did.

"I just worry about Haley," I tell him.

"Haley will be okay," Cash says.

"Holly will take care of her. That household was abusive just as much as Michael Berkley was." I nod, knowing that he's right. And I ruminate on his words some more as we hit the highway that will take us back to the interstate.

"You know," I say. "I went down there thinking all of this is insane." Cash looks over at me in the darkness. "But that night we were out in the woods with Katie," I say, shaking my head. "I can't get it out of my head. I think about what happened at my house and then this, and I can't stop thinking about either of them and both of them combined."

Cash smiles at me. The green glow of the c̲ minating his dimples. I go on.

"What else is out there?" I ask. "What else is real?"

"That's the question, isn't it?" he responds. I look back at the highway in front of us. I look at the stars in the sky. And I feel something akin to wonder. I feel something that I'm imagining might be what my father was always feeling. At least I hope it was. The question repeats in my mind, and my heart swells with the possibility.

What else is out there?

JOIN MY NEWSLETTER

Sign up now and get a free horror novella, The Body Snatchers. You'll also get updates, freebies, news about me and my dogs, plus book discounts and sales!

Sign up here:

https://BookHip.com/PZGBMZT

ALSO BY MARNIE VINGE

SHOP NOW

www.marniewritesthrillers.com

Psychological Thrillers

The Getaway

Swingers

For Rosie

I Remember Everything

Cold Blood

Women's Thrillers

The Way It Ends

What We Did That Night

Manspreader

The Blair Graves Files

The Haunting of Solomon House

The Holloway Hoax

The Vampire's Game

One Night in September

Short Horror Collections

Thicker Than Water

In Sheep's Clothing

The Reunion

Romance

Gunshy